NIGHT IN ALCATRAZ

And Other Uncanny Tales

JEAN HARKIN

Printed by Createspace in the United States of America
First edition 2016

This is a work of fiction. All characters are fictitious, with occasional references to actual persons who once shared our planet.

Grateful acknowledgment is made to the publications in which these stories first appeared, sometimes in slightly different form:

- *The Writers' Mill Journal, vol. 4* (" Night in Alcatraz," "Mummy Reunion," "Deer Charm," and "Cold Case");
- *The Writers' Mill Journal, vol. 3* ("Fossil Find");
- *The Writers' Mill Journal, vol. 2* ("Hoofbeats of Destiny");
- *The Writers' Mill Journal, vol. 1* ("Who is She Who Watches?").

Source for my interpretation of the Wishram (Oregon) legend is *Coyote Was Going There: Indian Literature of the Oregon Country* by Jarold Ramsey, University of Washington Press, 1999.

Grateful acknowledgment also to photographers who have given permission for the photographs in this book, besides the author's: Nancy Pilotte (page 2), John Harkin (page 28), and Zechmann photographers (page 42).

ISBN-13: 978-1534717206   ISBN-10: 153471720X

Designed and formatted by Sheila Deeth
Cover design by Patricia Burraston
Cover photography by Nancy Pilotte

Find Jean at https://www.goodreads.com/jeanatwritersmill

Dedicated to the Writers' Mill writers,
especially Sheila Deeth and Pati Burraston
and to my brother Charlie Luckett,
who suggested this book

CONTENTS

Section 1: Uncanny and Quirky

NIGHT IN ALCATRAZ

Under a full moon in San Francisco, I played Monopoly with my twelve-year old grandson. The house was quiet; everyone in the family had gone to bed an hour earlier. A clock ticked, the refrigerator clunked out ice cubes. Sycamore trees stirred, a branch tapping the windowpane. Parker slouched over his arm on the table. I drew a card: *Go to Jail*.

I heard Parker chuckle as I was transported into the indigo night through the bay window. The sky seemed starless, paled by the moon's brilliance. I flew so rapidly there was barely time to wonder: *Where am I going? Why, and by whose power?*

Out over dark waters, I could smell the salty, fishy air of San Francisco Bay and hear the slosh of white-crested waves as they rose and collapsed. I saw the Golden Gate Bridge in silhouette, like an eerie shadow on a blank wall.

A bank of fog rolled in from the open ocean, and I was carried along by a draft of air. Ahead I saw a deformation in the water's surface. I circled toward a lighthouse beacon that blinked at intervals, signaling to me. As I drew closer, I saw that the dark obstruction in the whitecaps was actually a stony promontory, an island occupied by a blocky building, bleached white as bones, with vacant windows.

I swooped in over the forbidding structure that seemed to have no entrance. Locked up tight and secure. I have no idea how I suddenly landed in a dismal space deep within its walls.

I was shoeless on bare, cold concrete in a room lit by moonbeams leaking through barred windows. I imagined gross things hiding among the shadows. I dared not move, lest I step on a giant cockroach, a furry rat, or something dead. I could smell rot, mold, blood, gunpowder. Why was I here? Oh yes, *Go to Jail*, the card commanded. What was my crime?

Through the windows I saw lights from the city on the mainland until the meandering fog dimmed my view. Voices carried across the water, and I felt the hopelessness and isolation of a prisoner doomed here, in view of life; freedom perhaps lost forever.

Within the garrison that enclosed me, I began hearing other sounds: Clanging of metal like tin cups striking iron bars, faint music from a banjo, far off laughter punctuated by an occasional scream. I shivered, wondering how long I would have to stay here. Had Parker sent me? Would he save me before going to bed?

My eyes gradually adapted to the darkness, and I tuned in to detect nearby sounds. I heard something like toenails on bricks, then shuffling. I was not alone, after all, in this lonely enclosure. Piercing the gloom, I saw a small gray cat near enough to touch. Looking again, I saw it wasn't a cat but a grimy-faced child in sooty clothes. Small, even for a child—a wraith perhaps.

"Can you help me?" it said.

"I don't know. I think I need help too—to get out of here. Where are we? Who are you?"

The Wraith seemed amused; I saw the sparkle of an eye. "Alcatraz Prison, of course. Are you just visiting?"

"I hope so." I smiled, wishing I had saved that *Get Out of Jail Free* card. "But who are you, and what are you doing here?"

"One question at a time," The Wraith whispered. "I'm lookin' for someone."

"Who?"

"A person from the past." I thought I detected an Irish accent when the word *person* came out like *parson*.

"How long ago?" I asked.

"Sommat less than a hundred years or so. Lost track a bit."

"Have you been here long? How did you get in?"

"No. Not long. Look at me—I can slip in anywhere—like smoke I can!" Indeed, the lithe little body could have passed through iron bars or a rat hole in the crumbling walls. "This here's me story," The Wraith continued. "Me father was here in this very room. At least his ghost was."

I tried to settle comfortably on the damp pavement and wrapped my arms around my knees, hugging myself for warmth, ready to listen to the creature's story.

"Me da's ghost came here to torment his murderer."

Fingers of mist stretched through the bars on the windows, and a dripping sound echoed from the walls, as The Wraith explained, "Me da was Myles O'Bannion, a florist by trade, in Chicago in the 1920s. A good man, but with a touch of the Irish temper in 'im. He gunned a man down once for no reason. Myles also liked his liquor and started his own brewery. A good trade that, but illegal." The Wraith giggled.

"His brewery deals needed some protectin', and that's when he got to know some of the Chicago operators like the Genna Brothers, Johnny Torrio, and Al Capone. Me da once tricked Torrio out of some money, and 'twas Torrio landed in jail. Torrio and his friend Capone didna take this lightly.

"In those days the crime bosses were doin' a good business in funerals too, and me father was florist of choice for Capone and his allies. In 1924 the head of Unione Siciliana in Chicago died, and Capone was in charge of funeral arrangements. He ordered a ton of flowers from Myles. When Capone's lads walked into me da's shop to shake hands on the flower deal, they pulled out guns and fired six shots into me da, killed him dead on the spot."

The Wraith stopped, as if listening for a sound from the prison's interior, then continued with the story. "After

Capone was sent here to Alcatraz for tax evasion, me da's ghost kept busy every night, visiting Capone's cell. Taunted him with flowers, booze, a gift, then pulled out a knife or machine gun to threaten him. Sometimes he'd play games and chase Capone around his wee cell, laughin' as his victim hollered for the guards to rescue 'im. Me father even showed up when Capone was isolated in the dreaded dark cell. No light a-shinin' there at all. But to Capone, there in the blackness, appeared the face of Myles O'Bannion, lit up like a jack o'lantern. I loved that scene!"

The Wraith chuckled hideously. "Now I'm here to carry on the tradition of Myles O'Bannion, God rest 'is soul. I'm searchin' for Al Capone or what's left of 'im."

I hesitated to disappoint my cellmate but thought it prudent to inform The Wraith, "I'm sure Capone died a long time ago. Went crazy in the end, I think."

At this, the creature cackled with glee, rolling over and over. Then it jumped up and announced, "We dance!"

The two of us began floating like ghosts through the corridors lined with heavily barred cells. As we bypassed the metal cages that once held trapped men, we heard shrieks, murmurs, and catcalls. Approaching the musty, dank-smelling shower room, we heard music—the tinkle of a banjo—coming from the end of the passageway. The tune was distinct, a joyful sound, as we entered the broad expanse of an open, un-private shower room. Moonlight flooded through the iron bars on the windows along one side of the room.

The Wraith cocked its head, listening. "He's here!"

"Who?"

"Capone—he's the banjo player, plays in the shower, dontcha know!"

The lively banjo music was deftly finger-picked, chord strummed. The Wraith moved across the rough floor to where moonlight concentrated in a circle of shimmering water droplets. My companion began to dance to the melody, stepping lightly, twirling, and kicking its heels in the style of a 1920s flapper.

I lost myself for a moment, enchanted with the dancing sprite in the glistening spotlight. I clapped my hands and began to sway to the jingly rhythm of the banjo tune.

The Wraith seemed happy, lost in the music, dancing merrily. I turned away, hoping to find my way out of this monstrous steel and concrete jungle. Following drafty corridors illuminated by moonlight flickering through windows on exterior walls, I tried to find a means of escape. Approaching the dining area, I heard the clamor of metal against metal, yells and laughter, and noticed the faint odor of stale coffee. Opposite the dining hall was a door marked *Recreation Yard*. I thought, at least a way outside! Of course, the door was locked. A sign nailed to the door read:

Games allowed:

Baseball, basketball

Bridge, Auto-Bridge, Chess, Checkers, Hearts

No gambling!

I said aloud, "I wonder if they played Monopoly." I hoped to find a *Get Out of Jail Free* card ….

A giggle interrupted me. The Wraith again! "'Tis not likely Monopoly was allowed here."

"Why not?"

"Too disruptive. I tell ye—the inmates, with all the temptations of wealth! And then the goin' to jail part."

"Oh, I see. But maybe the guards played Monopoly. I'd like to find a set with the *Get Out of Jail Free* card."

The Wraith scratched its head with a skeletal hand and started to speak, just as a tremendous whoosh and fluttering sound erupted at the dining hall windows. A massive shadow with multiple wings banged and charged against the barred panes. "A break-in!" chortled the little ghost.

I wasn't amused, but rather confused, dazed, and disoriented, as I'd been from the moment I entered Alcatraz. The arrival of vampires now wouldn't surprise me. Anything could happen!

The Wraith continued to grin and jump around with delight. "It's the canaries, bless their feathery souls! The Birdman's pets they wouldna let him keep."

I'd heard of Robert Stroud, the bird expert kept here on The Rock for seventeen years. "He didn't have his birds here with him?"

"No, indeed. Fer shame, the rules wouldna allow it."

The flapping and banging against the windows continued frantically. At last, glass shattered, and wind whistled through the crack. I shivered. "So why are they here? What can they want? The Birdman died long ago. Where did these birds come from?"

I expected a response from The Wraith, my ally in this strange predicament. But my companion had disappeared. Instead, a gray pigeon strutted past me into the dining hall. With a burst of wing power, the pigeon flung itself into the air toward the disturbance at the windows. And then, a swarm of canaries—yellow, rosy, indigo, green—streamed into the dining hall. I watched them flying in a pattern, dozens, hundreds of them, invading the prison, winging their way toward the corridors and cells, perfectly synchronized, none colliding. All was in flux, a beautiful flow of hundreds of rainbow-hued canaries. *Searching for what?*

As if on a signal, the flight pattern reversed itself, and the canaries rushed back into the dining hall. I ducked as the birds flew over me, like an airplane taking off. And then, I felt air beneath me; my feet no longer touching the floor. I was a featherweight, flying along with the canaries—out through the caged window without injury, and over the silent, dark waters of San Francisco Bay in the silvery moonlight. Off my right *wing*, I noticed the gray pigeon among the colorful little birds. I nodded, and the pigeon cocked its head. We heard cheering from behind us at The Rock.

My next sensation was a sharp tapping on my hand, and then a scratchy feeling against my knuckles. I looked. The Monopoly board still lay on the table between Parker and me. He was smiling and poking me with a *Get Out of Jail Free* card!

MUMMY REUNION

Halloween. A mellow orange light filtered through the tree limbs outside the window and cast a surreal glow over my living room. I felt a cold breath down my neck as the front door slammed shut.

I had just returned to the house after retrieving a single envelope from the mailbox. It lay brittle in my hand, the paper faded and smudged, bearing a 1994 postmark from Budapest. Who could have written me from Budapest over eighteen years ago? Although of Hungarian heritage, I had never known anyone in that country. The envelope had seen rough times. My curious fingers ripped it open, tearing a corner of the fragile contents. Slowing down to a more careful pace, I held my breath. A musty scent made me cough as I unfolded the page.

I couldn't have dreamed what I read in that letter:

June 21, 1994—Dear Orlavitz Descendant,

Your ancestors, Michael and Veronica Orlavitz, who died of tuberculosis in Vac, Hungary in 1786, along with their youngest child, Johannes, have virtually risen from the dead. Their well-preserved bodies in pine coffins were recently discovered in a forgotten church crypt in Vac. Except for insect bores in areas of the flesh, the bodies and clothing are well-preserved, probably due to the cool dry air in the crypt and oil released from the pine wood.

The outstanding condition of this deceased family qualifies them as mummies, due all possible respect. We suggest that you honor them with re-burial, either in their home village of Vac or, perhaps, in your own country. It is now possible for descendants to claim ownership of mummies and keep them at your own discretion, such as a donation to a museum or university setting, or in your own home. (To creep out friends and family?)

If we do not receive a reply from you within six months, we are authorized by the Government of Hungary to allow these bodies to be leased by the Mummies International organization that plans to tour various nations during the next twenty years. The exhibit will begin its Oregon visitation in Portland on November 2, 2012, ending in the summer of 2013.

Hoping to hear from you regarding your wishes in this matter ... Hungarian National History Museum.

Six months! Now, years too late to reply. *Mummies International,* coming *here* in two days—All Souls Day! Oh my god, my heart was thumping against my breastbone, hands quivering. I called out to my husband.

Jim sauntered in from elsewhere in the house. My hand shook as I handed him the letter. "I can't believe this—read it!"

His wide fingers clasped my forearm. "Steady as she goes," he said, quoting one of his sailing mottoes. His dark eyes held mine for a moment, as if to stabilize me; he took the letter. "What in the devil?" He shoved the paper at me and shrugged. "Some creepy Halloween prank. This isn't even English—it's some foreign language!"

"What!" I swallowed a breath. "It can't be. I read the whole thing just moments ago. It said—"

"How could you? It's in some strange language. It's—"

"Hungarian, perhaps? But Jim, I could read it when I opened it." I looked again at the letter. No, not in English anymore! It's a good thing I had read carefully the first time, as I was able to rattle off what I remembered of the baffling message from the past.

Jim stared at me for a moment under his bushy caterpillar eyebrows. Then he stretched his clasped hands above his head and cracked his knuckles. "Maybe it's your Hungarian DNA affecting your subconscious. Who knows!" Un-stretching, he turned to leave the room, then shot back, "Or that goulash we ate for dinner last night!"

Some things are just too weird for Jim to take seriously. I gazed down at the letter and felt that chilly breath on my neck again.

* * *

I could hardly wait! November 2 was a sunny day, no sign of ghostly clouds or eerie fog to mar the weather. I set out by myself to view *Mummies International* the day it opened in Portland. If I were to find anything interesting, Jim agreed he'd return with me for a second look.

The line at the Oregon Museum of Science and Industry (OMSI) was long and slow at late morning, as families had trouble deciding which exhibits, films, and attractions to view. Finally, my turn at the ticket counter went quickly, as I had one thing on my mind—to view the mummy exhibit. "Movie too?" the clerk inquired.

"No thanks, just the mummies."

Did the air grow chill as I rode the escalator to the exhibit entrance? Too-good air conditioning, I surmised.

The entrance to *Mummies International* led into a large enclosure shrouded by heavy draperies the color of midnight. Immediately, the outside world of sunshine and excited voices in the museum was snuffed out. I waited in a gloomy cavern with a line of ten other tourists. In the dark, no one spoke, as we waited for our gray-haired guide to usher us in. After moments of anticipation, the man spoke in a hushed voice, reminding us to conduct ourselves with respect for the dead. With a swooping motion, he opened the curtain, allowing us to enter the hall of mummies. The adults entered cautiously while three children pushed ahead, pointing and whispering.

Rows of glass cases on varnished wood pedestals housed the mummies. Each display was labeled with information about the enclosed remains. I quickly learned that mummies are not always of the Egyptian type. Many were accidentally preserved, in contrast to the carefully prepared burials of the pharaohs. A Peruvian infant, brown with age, was a thousand years older than King Tut; a black-haired Chilean woman with tattoos still visible on her leathery breasts was yet two thousand years older than the Egyptian boy king.

Not all of the mummies were human. A white-boned squirrel, devoid of hair, had died and dried up in an attic. A dog mummy had been preserved in a peat bog. A Howler monkey, clothed in a skirt of white feathers, had been prepared after death by loving hands. It looked alarmingly alive.

As I peered into the rectangular glass cases at the hollow visages and awkward joints under nearly transparent skin of the dead, living faces gazed back from the other three sides. Their expressions ranged from curious and awed, to horrified and grossed out; occasionally I saw a smile of understanding as viewers discussed what they saw.

Flickering lights of a video screen across the room drew me to a time-sequenced presentation of how once-living things decay. The vegetables succumbing to moldy gray fuzz—I'd seen that before in my own refrigerator. A dead bunny melted into the ground, leaving a hummock of soft white fur. But the decaying rat, swelling with rot, was more than I could stomach. I turned away.

I had seen almost enough but was disappointed not to have found my ancestors, the Orlavitz family, among the exhibits. It was time to escape from the funereal and solemn into the light of ordinary life and maybe find something to eat in the OMSI cafeteria.

I snuck out from between the curtains, once again into the dim entrance foyer. As I headed to the exit, a voice stopped me. "May I help you?" It came from a statue-still man standing in a corner beside the exit. I couldn't see his face well in the darkness, but I perceived he was wearing a weird usher-like jacket with three rows of buttons down the front.

"Is this the way to the cafeteria?" I asked. I caught the aroma of pizza, wafting.

"If you leave, you cannot return." His monotone voice was formal. Zombie-like, perfect for the mummies' exhibit.

"Well, I think I'm done. I've seen enough."

"Have you been upstairs?" A bony finger emerged from his sleeve and pointed upward. I hadn't noticed the stairs before and didn't know there was a second level to the exhibit. "You will find the European mummies on the second level," the man said in his hollow voice.

"Really? I didn't know. Thanks."

I climbed the stairs, thinking that European mummies might well include my long-dead ancestors. The second floor contained more glass cases with mummies, their stories posted on two sides of each display. There were at least as many glass tombs here as on the lower level. I took a breath and began searching the hall of the dead.

After gazing at a well-preserved 18th century German nobleman with his boots still on, I moved to the next case. There lay a female mummy with shriveled bare feet, wearing an ankle-length dress with an apron. The display card revealed her name—Veronica Orlavitz, my ancestor! I stared; Veronica stared back with her empty eyes and slack jaw. Hard to believe she was only thirty-eight years old!

Next to sun-bonneted Veronica was a baby-sized display case containing her infant son Johannes. He was laid out on a pristine white sheet. The tiny mummy wore a cap with crocheted trim around his face and on the seams of the crown. His little jacket had triangular scallops at the waist; below that he wore a pin-striped skirt over bloomers tied at the ankles. How sweet he must have been!

My family! I almost cried, reading about their lives and how they'd all been sickened and died with tuberculosis in the late 18th century.

The case next to Johannes's was full-sized, slightly longer than Veronica's. Michael Orlavitz's name was on the label, but the case was empty, the white-sheeted pallet unoccupied. Where was Michael?

I felt a familiar chilly breath on my neck and someone tapping my shoulder. I turned to see a leathery pockmarked face stretched taut over cheekbones, vacant eye sockets, and broken teeth protruding from an open mouth. I recognized the rows of gold buttons and braid on the uniform. *The man from downstairs!*

I screamed. Then, I must have fainted. The high ceiling blurred before my eyes as people scurried around; hands lifted me to a sitting position. Someone offered water from a bottle. "Where's Michael?" I sputtered.

"What did she say?"

I said it louder, "Where's Michael?" A woman wearing an OMSI badge helped me stand. Then I looked over toward Michael Orlavtiz's glass enclosure and saw him lying there—all stretched out in his blue embroidered uniform with three rows of gold buttons down the front. The sleeves and trousers were decorated with loops of heavy braid. In his skeletal hands he embraced an ornate silver Christian cross. His vacant gaze held the ceiling.

Who would believe that the mummified Michael Orlavitz had talked to me and had, a few moments ago, tapped me on the shoulder! Certainly not my husband Jim!

Would you?

COLD CASE

It was the 1940s. Mornings when the dairy truck rattled the silence off dawn, and people joked that the latest newborn in the neighborhood looked just like the milkman. But the story I remember about our milkman is an eerie one:

Roy, everyone's friendly milkman, made his rounds one warm, dewy morning in June. Drops of water ran off the bottles of milk as the steamy air condensed the cold moisture. Roy jerked his truck to a stop at the curb of Mrs. Morgan's house. Crisp in all-white shirt and pants, Roy leaped out from his long door and sprinted to the front porch, droplet-splashed bottles clinking in a metal carrier. He knew what Mrs. Morgan usually ordered—two quarts of milk on each delivery day, and if she wanted eggs, butter, cream or other products, she'd leave him a message in one of her returned quart bottles.

Roy placed the full milk bottles next to the Morgans' front door and reached for the empties to replace in his carrier. Picking up one bottle, he saw a note enclosed. It read: *Please Help!* Roy stared at the note. Should he ring the doorbell? It was only 5:30 in the morning. He wondered if this were a joke. *Probably a kid's idea*. He chuckled, somewhat relieved at the thought, and tucked the note into his shirt pocket. He took a good look at the heavy green front door, just to assure himself it looked secure with no evidence of break-in, and returned to his morning rounds.

Two days later, Roy again approached Mrs. Morgan's house. He felt an extra beat in his heart and took a deep breath as his quick feet sprang up the steps and along the sidewalk to the front porch. He shot a quick look at the empty bottles as he placed the new order. No messages!

Roy breathed a deep sigh. *Must've been the kids!* He shook his head.

Another two weeks and four more deliveries went by, with Mrs. Morgan's only messages being an occasional *one dozen eggs, please Roy* or *I need cream today.* Roy always noticed her backward handwriting as it resembled his own. He thought she must be a lefty too.

All seemed normal along Palmdale Avenue until a morning near the end of June. It was another muggy morning when milk could curdle quickly. Roy was stepping lively in his rounds until he reached Mrs. Morgan's front door and found a short urgent message in a quart bottle: *Please help now!* Roy sucked in his lips. *Darn kids! What fun is this?* He wondered what reaction the kids were expecting. He didn't even know these kids—their ages, gender, how many were there? Some spoiled, pimply-faced brat who drank a quart of milk every day? A couple of giggly siblings imagining a milkman's confusion? He shook his head, put the note in his pocket, and retreated to the truck.

Two days later Roy discovered another note in one of Mrs. Morgan's empty bottles. *Roy, please help me NOW!* This one seemed personal, with his name included, and the NOW in all caps. He thought of leaving a note for Mrs. Morgan and asking her to call off the kids. He felt for a pen in his shirt pocket. No luck. Next time he'd carry a pen, in case this happens again.

A week later—in mid-July—Roy felt a little easier in that two deliveries had taken place without notes. But this time: *It's happening. Please, please help me!* When Roy looked at the door he noticed a scuffmark. Mrs. Morgan's door and front porch had always been pristine. He touched the door to see if it would yield. It was shut tight. He thought better of leaving a note for Mrs. Morgan and decided to alert the police instead. *That would show those kids a thing or two!*

The police followed up on Roy's call. When Roy explained the situation on the phone to Sergeant Lewis, the policeman asked Roy to save the help messages he'd received as possible evidence, "just in case something turns up." His hearty chuckle bothered Roy. "Of course it's probably a kids' joke, like you say." Roy promised to retrieve as many of the messages he could find; some were still tucked in his pockets.

Two mornings later, Roy's truck was loaded and ready to leave the dairy for the morning rounds. Before taking off, he stepped into the office to say a few words to Marjorie, the big red-haired dispatcher/receptionist who had just returned from her vacation. At the same time, a runt of a boy wearing a golfer's cap burst into the office with his load of morning newspapers. The boy could barely contain his excitement as he slapped a newspaper on the counter in front of Marjorie. "Look at this!" he shrieked. In bold block print, the headline packed a wallop: *Jessica Morgan Murdered in Her Bed.*

"Let me see!" Roy knocked the boy aside as he grabbed a paper for himself. "My customer—Mrs. Morgan!" Roy moaned and immediately felt faint. Marjorie and the boy watched Roy try to read the story aloud. His hands rattled the newspaper, and his arms shook all the way to his shoulders. His voice began to fail, so Marjorie proceeded with the story. Roy heard some of it:

"... Suffocated with her pillow ... signs of a struggle ... no suspects ... Mrs. Morgan lived alone. There was no one else living in the home, and no sign of a break-and-entry." Beginning the final paragraph, Marjorie hesitated and looked at Roy. "It says here the police are investigating a local milkman's story that notes of distress were left in her empty milk bottles during the past six weeks to two months." Marjorie put down the newspaper. "Oh Roy! Was that you?"

Roy nodded. "I don't feel so good just now."

Marjorie swung around to Roy's side of the counter. She motioned to the newsboy—"Grab that chair!" To the milkman: "Sit down, Roy. You don't look so good either."

Roy sank onto the wooden straight chair. "I'll call a substitute driver for you. You can't go out there today."

Roy rubbed his head with both hands and murmured, "Thanks, Marjorie."

* * *

Roy was arrested and indicted for the murder of Mrs. Morgan. The police had suspected him of writing the notes left in the bottles. His fingerprints were found on the front door. No one but Mrs. Morgan lived in the house (she had no children), and there was no forced entry. It was thought that the woman could have opened the door to Roy. He had acted guilty in not making his rounds the morning after the murder. Roy was not a white man, so therefore he drew suspicion.

Roy was acquitted at the trial due to lack of motive and no fingerprints or other evidence on the body or surroundings that could be linked to Roy. He was never seen in the neighborhood again, and no one knew whether he continued working at the dairy. Most people assumed he had left town, or they didn't care to know. Roy would be in his late eighties or nineties by now if he were still alive. No other person was ever accused or brought to trial for the murder of Mrs. Morgan. The crime remains a mystery to this day.

THE TRADITIONAL LEGEND

Long ago, before humans became real people, Coyote the Trickster came up the great river to change things. According to a Wishram legend, Coyote visited a village and asked the inhabitants if they were living well. The people sent the trickster god to see their chief, Tsagaglalal (She Who Watches) who lived high up on the rocks above the river. Even though Coyote learned she was a kind leader, teaching her people to live well and build sturdy houses with roofs made of reed mats, he warned her that the world would soon change, with women no longer permitted to be leaders. He said to Tsagaglalal: "You will cease to be a chief." Coyote then changed her into a boulder and commanded her to stay there and "Keep watch over the people living in this place." To this day, Tsagaglalal's large eyes are watching.[1]

[1] Paraphrased from source: Ramsey, Jarold, ed. *Coyote Was Going There,* "Tsagigla'lal" p. 53. Seattle and London: University of Washington Press, 1999.

WHO IS SHE WHO WATCHES?

A personal re-interpretation of
the traditional Wishram legend

When the sumac was in full scarlet cloak, swirling along the canyon walls near the Wishram village, the tribal chief Tsagaglalal—She Who Watches—came down from her little house high on the cliff where she lived with Cat Woman. The two companions often wandered and climbed the rocky walls together above the quiet community. This October day, with smoke of salmon-drying fires rising straight up into the blue sky, She Who Watches left Cat Woman basking in the sunshine to investigate something unusual her watching eyes had spotted floating westward down the river.

In her eagle-feather headdress, Tsagaglalal hurried by the villagers in their busy occupations—pounding roots, repairing stone tools and dip nets, drying salmon on scaffolds, making rain capes from cedar bark. The people looked up and warmly greeted the good chief as she passed. Tsagaglalal had done well by her followers, and the settlement enjoyed a peaceful, fruitful existence that even afforded time for leisurely pursuits. Some tribal members liked to draw story pictures and symbols of their lives on the lichen-kissed basalt rocks along the gorge of the great river.

Carrying her basket, Tsagaglalal reached the riverbank and shielded her eyes to the morning sun. She looked upriver and saw several crude dugout canoes approaching with mostly white-faced men aboard. Among the travelers was one black-faced man, dark as a tree; a woman in Shoshone clothing with a baby strapped to her back; and a large, shaggy, black dog, eagerly watching the river float by. The panting dog with a strong, broad head suddenly jumped from the leading canoe into the icy water and swam over to greet Tsagaglalal—She Who Watches. She laughed as the dog came ashore and shook off an explosion of water droplets. As soon as the boatmen could reach the bank, Tsagaglalal began to welcome the friendly but travel-worn crew. She happily greeted the woman traveler who identified herself as Bird Woman and her baby boy, Pomp. Tsagaglalal—She Who Watches—reached into her cedar basket and gave Bird Woman one of her eagle feathers, then was introduced to the two captains who were leading the mission for the Great White Father far across many mountains.

A few curious Wishram folk also came over to meet the strangers, who smelled of spoiled elk meat and rotting leather, and wanted to touch the hand of the large dark-skinned man with bright eyes. The people offered salmon to their visitors, but the boat riders refused the Wishrams' esteemed delicacy. The villagers were a little insulted, somewhat amused, by the strangers' preference for spoiled elk over salmon. But Tsagaglalal, as chief of the Wishram, ignored this rebuff and conferred with the white-skinned chiefs about their plans. She learned they were heading to the ocean. Traveling onward, they would soon hear the thunder of Celilo Falls.

The voyagers had been advised by the people upriver to portage around the falls. But as that tribe had stolen from them and played many jokes, the white-faces paid little heed to their warning. She Who Watches rose to her full authoritarian stature, shook her head, and said they must avoid Celilo Falls. It was a churning chasm of white water disrupting the mighty Columbia and would surely sweep them mercilessly to the bottom of the river. She warned that members of the Wasco, farther along the river, would be waiting to salvage whatever supplies bobbed up to the surface. She Who Watches looked pityingly at Bird Woman, Pomp, and the dog. I must save them, she thought.

The captains conferred and seemed to accept Tsagaglalal's counsel. Several members of the group went ashore with their canoes, provisions, and valuable instruments, preparing to skirt the falls by land. But they were in a hurry to arrive at the Pacific Ocean without further delay, so the majority of the travelers pushed back toward the center of the broad river. The one named Captain Lewis waved to the shore party. "See you on the other side!"

Tsagaglalal was not happy with what was taking place and knew that if the maelstrom of Celilo Falls didn't drown the group, Short Narrows—a chute of raging water leading out of the rapids through gate-like cliffs—would surely claim them all. Immediately, She Who Watches turned herself into an eagle, and her feather headdress flew her aloft toward Celilo Falls to save the ill-fated voyagers.

As Tsagaglalal hovered above the white captains and their company in the fragile canoes (so inferior to the Wishrams' own canoes), she summoned Wy-Kan-Ush-Mi Wa-Kish-Wit, the Spirit of the Salmon, and turned all the travelers into salmon for their passage over the perilous falls and rapids. The moment before they were transformed, Bird Woman and her baby thought they heard an eagle's cry above them, but it was Tsagaglalal laughing at her own magic—"Now the chiefs who refused to eat salmon must swim as salmon!"

When the last of the fish people had shot through the falls and the shattering rapids, She Who Watches changed them back into people riding their canoes; and she flew homeward. As Tsagaglalal glanced back over her wings, she saw the dog looking skyward at her; and she heard the joyous yells and hoots of the voyagers celebrating their survival.

While She Who Watches was away on her life-saving mission, the trickster Coyote approached her little house high on the rocks above the Wishram village. Only Cat Woman was at home. When she saw Coyote coming near, she blinked in the sun—*I will play a trick on that sly devil himself!* As Coyote bounded his way up the rocky slope, Cat Woman stood up, stretched her spine from head to toe, and mused, "This time the laugh is on Coyote." She slipped inside Tsagaglalal's little house.

* * *

After Coyote's visit, the Wishram people ran into their houses in great fear of the large burnt-red face on a rock that suddenly appeared above their settlement, staring down at them with great soul-seeking eyes. The people did not understand Cat Woman's trickery and did not know what had actually occurred high up on the rocks. They believed Coyote had placed an awful spell on their good chief Tsagaglalal.

She Who Watches returned from saving the white-faces and their companions and walked proudly into the village. When her frightened people saw Tsagaglalal, they surrounded her with hugs of joy, tears of relief, and told her excitedly of Coyote's visit. Tsagaglalal climbed up to see the face on the rock that had appeared near her home during her brief absence. As she approached the reddish rock face with features drawn in white—many circles outlining large eyes—Tsagaglalal began to laugh. Her piercing eagle laugh rang out and bounced off the dark rocks surrounding the village. She sank down on a grassy perch under the bewitched rock and laughed harder and harder, holding her sides. She Who Watches saw that the image imprisoned in the rock was not her likeness at all. There were dainty ears above the round eyes and a nose, too delicate to be hers. Tsagaglalal realized at once what had happened: Cat Woman had stood in for her when Coyote came to pay his visit and play his tricks. Instead, Cat Woman had deceived Coyote and preserved Tsagaglalal's benevolent leadership for the tribe.

Today if you go to view the petroglyphs and rock paintings at Columbia Hills State Park (at Horse Thief Lake) near Wishram, Washington, you will see the face of She Who Watches on a high rock. But take a closer look and see the face of a cat—not a woman—keeping watch over the beautiful Columbia River Gorge.

DEER CHARM

"My child! Come out ... come out ... come out!" These were the words my daughter heard as she stumbled out of bed to walk on planked flooring toward the door of our cabin. Jenny, not a sleepwalker, told me she'd heard those words distinctly, as I hugged her soft shoulder to steady her. Her hair was matted with sweat, and her eyes struggled to stay open. In the first light of dawn, I noticed that the deer charm necklace she had insisted on wearing to bed was no longer around her neck, but that detail could wait for morning. The floor creaked as I ushered Jenny back to her single bed. I heard one of the boys toss in his sleep and Jack, my husband, quietly snoring. I climbed back onto my cot and lay there awhile, unable to stop thinking about the bizarre coincidence of Jenny's and my dreams.

Jenny's bumbling about had awakened me from a nightmare in which someone was trying to kidnap her from our room. In my dream I had gotten out of bed to protect my daughter and had become involved in a tug-of-war against a hooded stranger whose features I couldn't see. Jenny was between us, and I had her by one finger, with the shadowy figure winning over. It was then I heard the floorboards squeak and Jenny moaning. How odd we'd been experiencing a similar dream episode! I would ask her more about it in the morning.

I couldn't get back to sleep. There we were in a cabin on stilts, part of a hotel resort perched on a high bluff within view of the empty cliff houses and hanging towers of the Ancient Ones—the Anasazi—who had inhabited Mesa Verde centuries ago. I recalled our first sight of this ruin ….

Yesterday morning, our route had followed along the Colorado River, and then gradually began to climb, leaving the river rushing to its own destination below us. As we drove along the Colorado Plateau, I suddenly saw the panorama of Mesa Verde clinging to an opposite canyon wall. "Look! Jack, can you pull over?" I began to dive for the camera in my tote bag.

I heard Paul in the far back seat of our van. "Wow!"

And from Chris, "Double wow!" Then some tussling between the boys, as Jack steered over to a scenic overlook pullout.

Jenny peered out her window through the binoculars. "Mom, it's amazing! Seeing it with my own eyes, it's so—"

"Real!" supplied Chris. He giggled as Paul punched him. But I knew what Jenny meant. Low clouds gliding through the canyon gave a shimmering effect to the stone-walled cliff dwelling with its hollow windows, rooms and towers open to the sky. The effect was of a Disneyesque kingdom suspended from sheer red rock walls.

"Can you believe people actually lived there, back before Columbus discovered America?" I said.

"They must have been good climbers," commented Paul.

"Better than you," piped Chris. More tussling.

"Boys!"

Jack spoke. "Those people suddenly abandoned the cliff homes over six hundred years ago. No one knows for sure why they left."

"Something bad happened," said Jenny.

"Like what?" asked Chris.

"Just a guess. How should I know!"

"Jenny's right," I said. "It had to be something pretty terrible to chase them out after living there for centuries."

We continued speculating and discussing as Jack started us back on the road, heading southwest toward the Four Corners and the Navajo reservation.

As we rolled along the two-lane highway, I ignored the boys in the back seat and watched the high desert landscape slide by, as did Jenny. Jack hummed to himself and quick-looked at bits of the scenery. Pinon pines straggled along the route, finding niches to grow among the sandstone boulders. Sheep grazing close to the roadsides made similar shapes to the fuzzy cholla cactus as we sped by.

A hawk floated on circling air currents above the dry, red landscape. I lowered my window to hear its slurring whistle, and the scent of hot pavement rushed into our cool car. I looked back at Jenny as the sudden gust lifted the bangs off her forehead. "Mom, why did you open the window?" inquired Paul.

"Did you hear the hawk?"

"Maybe." Back to chattering with his brother.

A road sign alerted us to *Kayenta Market Today—Four Corners.* "Can we stop there, Dad?" Jenny whined as if she expected him to decline.

"Yep," he responded. It was definitely time for a break.

We followed the signs to the market venue. No wonder I'd noticed few cars on the highway—they had already converged on the Kayenta Market—just as four southwestern states had come together at this meeting point.

An assortment of tourists' cars and dust-covered pickups marked the site of the Navajo reservation's marketplace. Native women in long skirts and men in skinny jeans lured prospective buyers to check out their handicrafts, displayed on blankets spread on the ground. Silver and turquoise jewelry glinted in the sunshine. Shoppers unfolded blankets of red, black, and white with bold designs. Smoke from cooking pots curled through the air, and I knew my family would not leave hungry. As we passed by her station, I smiled at a middle-aged Navajo woman at a weaving loom. Two young boys with raven black, fly-away hair played beside her.

"Mom, look!" Jenny kept repeating and poking me as we gawked at every craftsman's presentation. The sprawl and sparkle of all the Navajo jewelry and artisan crafts were too overwhelming for me to focus on buying any one item. But Jenny was different. She wanted everything!

I reminded her, "Dad will want to get back on the road, so we can't stay too long."

"Okay." As Jenny reached down to pick up a ring—a turquoise oval set in burnished silver—an old woman approached.

"You need charm," the woman said.

"Excuse me?" Jenny replied. The woman extended a long, weathered hand on which dangled a silver necklace bearing a single charm, so bright it blinked white in the sun.

"Oh! It's lovely. What is it?" Jenny replaced the turquoise ring on the blanket and attended to the silver necklace and charm.

"You need this," the woman said, drawing her apple-doll face close to Jenny's. I noticed that for an old face, the woman's eyes were young and brilliantly dark, with long lashes. She smelled of earth and wood smoke.

"I need it?" Jenny seemed puzzled.

"Children need deer charm." The silver charm was a delicately sculpted deer with two tiny antlers curving upward. The old woman, with gray strands twined among her black hair, allowed Jenny to touch the charm. Jenny's approval shone in her eyes.

"Why do children need this?" I intervened. Jenny, at thirteen, was quickly leaving childhood behind.

"Protection," hissed the woman. Jenny jumped as the woman spat the word.

"From what?"

"You've heard of La Llorana!" This was not a question.

"No, not really," I said.

"La Llorana have many shapes. Sometime deer, sometime old woman, sometime mother who lost children.

She an Ancient One. Enemy come, children lost. La Llorana search for children, take them back."

"And the charm?" I asked.

"Protect child, protect daughter." The woman was pushing the necklace into Jenny's hand. "Only ten dollar."

Jenny was not up to resisting such a hard sell. She looked at me. "Can I, Mom? I've got ten dollars."

"Never mind. I'll buy it for you." Then I laughed. "It's cheap insurance against La Llorana."

"And just beautiful." Jenny smiled at the woman, who cackled, revealing broken teeth. She tucked the money into her skirt pocket.

"You put on now," said the woman. Jenny bowed her head and let the woman's blackened fingers clasp the deer charm necklace around her throat. "You safe now. La Llorana not take you."

As we walked away in search of Jack and the boys, Jenny said, "Mom, did you see her feet?" I'd observed most of the Navajo matron but not her feet. "When she was fastening the necklace, I looked down and saw—like hooves sticking out from her skirt."

I had to laugh. "Probably just some pointy black shoes."

"Maybe. But they sure looked like hooves."

Weaving through the crowd of shoppers and Navajo families, Jack and the boys approached. They were loaded down with food—lunch for all of us, it looked like.

"Yum," beamed Chris. "Navajo tacos!"

"And I've got Kneel Down bread," chimed Paul, showing us a sort of cornbread tamale wrapped in a cornhusk.

"Ew," said Jenny. "Anything easier to eat?"

"I've got lots," said Jack, holding out a paper sack. "Plain fry bread, more tacos, pine nuts—let's find a table somewhere."

"And something to drink," added Chris.

That was our lunch and shopping break. In the afternoon, we left the Four Corners and headed toward Mesa Verde for a short, guided tour of the ancient ruins, and on to Cortez for our night's lodging. Jenny occasionally looked down at her charm necklace and fondled it, but nothing more was said about the strange woman, her myth about La Llorana, nor the protection of the deer charm.

At night in our lofty cabin (the whole place shook when anyone walked up or down the outside stairs), we chose our respective beds—all in the main room. The boys chose the bunk beds, and both, naturally, wanted the top bunk. Jack flipped a quarter to see who got the coveted berth. Paul, the twelve-year-old won the toss, claiming, "It's only fair—I'm older!"

The rest of us slept on single beds with inch-deep mattresses. We were ready to sleep hard after a day on the road and in the dry, sunny air. As Jenny scooted under her bed sheets, I suggested, "Don't you want to take off your necklace for sleeping?"

Her eyes sparkled as she touched the charm, "No, Mom. It's like a guardian spirit."

"Oh right," I said. Cozy, enclosed by handcrafted log walls, we turned out the lights. The moon winked a final good night through our window facing the ancient dwellings. Our family lay in peaceful slumber ….

Until Jenny's sleepwalking episode and my parallel nightmare that she was being pulled toward the cabin door by a kidnapper. And Jenny hearing that summons from a wailing voice in the night, "My child, come out!"

Morning light and heat came early—soon after I fell back to sleep, it seemed. The boys virtually leaped out of bed, wrestling and pillow fighting. I heard Jack's razor buzzing in the bathroom. Jenny and I could have used more sleep. I got off my cot, exhausted.

Jenny, in her rumpled summer pajamas, sat on the edge of her bed. She wasn't happy. "My finger hurts, and it's swollen. Look!" She pointed an index finger toward me, and indeed it was red and bulging around the knuckle.

"I'll get some ice from the fridge." I remembered the tug-of-war in my dream. Looking at Jenny's puffy eyes and frowny expression, I decided not to mention my dream just yet. Then I noticed again—"Jenny! Did you take off your necklace during the night? Do you remember sleepwalking?"

Jenny felt for the necklace at her throat. "It's gone! And I don't sleepwalk!"

"You did!"

She panicked and began tearing through her bed covers and pillow. "Where is it? My beautiful necklace!" She moaned, becoming tearful.

"Jenny, settle down. It's here someplace. You wore it to bed."

She was near screaming. "I know, Mom! Where can it *be*?" She tossed her pillow on the floor and stomped on it. By then, the commotion had attracted Paul and Chris.

"I'll look under your bed," said Chris, already on hands and knees. "Hey—there's a hole in the floor!" He stretched out his legs and lay belly-down to peer through the hole. "There's something down there on the ground!"

"Let me see." Jenny joined her brother beneath the bed, pushing him aside. "It's my charm necklace! Oh Mom, I have to go get it!"

"Not in your pajamas. Get dressed first," I said.

Paul had jumped into his jeans and was ready to rush down the stairs to retrieve Jenny's treasure. "Right back!" he called, exiting the cabin and thundering down the outside stairs. In less than two minutes he came racing back upstairs, shaking our quarters again. He burst in, holding Jenny's necklace, which she snatched immediately with a quick thank you. But I could see that the recovered property was not the cause of Paul's red-faced excitement. "Something was down there last night!" he shouted.

Jack emerged from the bathroom, toweling his face and smelling like a pine tree. "What did you see?"

"Tracks! I saw tracks under our room!"

"Better have a look, hadn't we!" said Jack. "As soon as I get dressed." He raised an eyebrow in my direction, and I shrugged.

"I'm going too," stated Chris.

I felt a chill, thinking of the mysterious dream episodes that had transpired in the night.

Jenny and I dressed to go out for breakfast, while Jack and the boys descended under the cabin to investigate. We heard Jack's calm voice and the boys' excited ones below us. "Jenny," I began, deciding it was time to collect and compare our nightmare experiences. "Sit down a minute." I motioned for her to come over to my cot. "Do you remember your dream last night when you got out of bed?" She started to answer, just as our guys returned.

"Deer tracks," Jack reported

"Yeah—all over the place," added Chris.

"And the scrub and grass all matted down like a deer slept there!" Paul said.

"Jenny," I continued my questioning of her reverie, "who called you to leave the cabin last night?" The boys and Jack stood at attention.

"I don't know," said Jenny in a small voice. "It was just a voice calling *my child, come out!*"

"La Llorana in her deer form?" I ventured.

"What?" said Chris, screwing up his face.

"We'll talk about this over breakfast," I said. "Let's go down to the café right now, but first you can show us the deer tracks."

We tromped
       down the
            shuddering
                  staircase....

A WINDOW AT NYE BEACH

2013

"Summer cottages built in the thirties or forties," said the art gallery clerk in answer to my inquiry. "They'll be torn down this year to make way for new businesses," she added, handing me a pen to sign my credit card receipt. With the usual "Have a nice day," "You too," Jack and I were out of the gallery and onto the sunny sidewalk with my newest art treasure from the Dazzling Frog boutique. Jack flipped on his sunglasses for our further sleuthing of the wonders of Nye Beach, Newport, Oregon.

We walked south on Coast Street that parallels the ocean a couple blocks away. We passed a women's clothing boutique at the corner, then crossed the side street and continued past a restaurant, its sign eclipsed by rhododendrons. Then another tempting boutique window, a bookstore, and a café with flowers in hanging baskets and two tables set outdoors. On the other side of the café lay a vacant lot, and beyond stood the two cottages that had piqued my curiosity.

As we passed the vacant lot, a strong breeze from the ocean pushed through, redolent of salt and fish, and crossing the weedy lot, the wind picked up a scent of old, dank earth. The two cottages were identical, once painted white, now weathered gray with spots of mold; green trim around the windows was peeling to the raw wood. A mailbox on a post remained in front of one cottage, rusty and gaping for mail undelivered since—when? Both front doors held *Do Not Enter* notices. "Looks like good homes for mice," said Jack. I cringed and made a frowny face, imagining how a house full of mice would smell.

A seagull screeched and flapped under the brilliant azure sky as we turned the corner, heading for the beach after a brief stop at our hotel. The sidewalk led along the side of the corner cottage and its forlorn backyard. The windows of the house were low enough to look inside, so I veered across a thin strip of weedy side yard to peer into the back window. Jack remained standing on the sidewalk.

I cupped my hands to block the daylight as I peered through the window. As my eyes adjusted to the darker interior, I made out the remnants of faded wallpaper—maybe once yellow with stripes of some kind of design—now beige and crumbling with water stains and mold. I saw a skittering motion across the baseboard of the far wall. "Yikes—it's a mouse!"

Jack laughed. "I told you!"

I looked and noticed more: A strand of ivy snaked across the dusty, bare floor from the near wall all the way to the closet and continued vining up the doorframe. "Look at this!" I turned to Jack and motioned him to the window. "Did you bring the camera?"

"Yep, right here," he said, fumbling in his pants pocket.

"Weird! Can you get a good picture of this ivy growing inside a house?"

Jack removed his sunglasses and folded them into his shirt pocket. "Well, there's a lot of contrast," he said. At that moment, a cloud cast a shadow, and a seagull flew over, cackling in descending tones. "He's laughing at us," Jack noted.

As he adjusted and framed the camera in several angles and vigorously clicked the shutter, I wondered how ivy could grow and thrive across the floor of a long-vacant, dry, empty room in search of the supporting doorway of the closet. "How can it live?" I said.

"Must be water somewhere—in the foundation. I'd guess that's where it's growing from." Jack captured some views of the mysterious ivy, we finished gawking, and then headed on our way ….

1939

A nine-year-old girl, with freckles and sunny brown hair in pigtails stood in the bedroom she shared with her little brother. They had both liked their mother's choice of the yellow wallpaper with vertical rows of seashell designs. She looked out the window and watched seagulls soaring and calling from the sky. Sunrays angling across the window and shining on her face made her feel warm and comfortable; she felt her sore throat healing in the sunshine and smiled. That day she was content to stay home alone while her parents and brother went off for some recreation at the Nye Creek Natatorium.

She remembered Mommy's cool hand on her forehead that morning, her mother's concerned frown as she said, "I think you should stay home this time. Summer colds are the worst." The girl didn't fret; she felt tired and preferred to curl up on her single bed, under her quilt, and read the latest adventure of Laura Ingalls and her pioneer family. Mommy had assured her, "You'll be all right by yourself for a little while. We won't stay long. The nice grandmother next door is home if you need anything."

Soon after, her parents and brother Charlie went off to swim or roller skate at the natatorium. The girl hadn't asked which they would do that day. She hadn't cared, in her eagerness to return to the next chapter about the pioneer girl who settled on *Plum Creek*. It wasn't long, however, before the sun warming the window and the coziness of the colorful crazy-quilt caused the girl to close her feverish eyes and let the book slide off the bed to the floor, landing quietly on a soft wool rug.

When she awoke, the sun no longer radiated in the room, and the sky was a purplish color. Rumbling in the atmosphere made her jump with surprise. The cries of the seagulls sounded alarms. She hopped out from under the quilt and ran to the window. The grumbling from the sky grew louder, and suddenly it seemed like a bucket of rainwater was thrown at the house and ran down the windowpane. She heard rain pounding the rooftop, and the deluge at the window blurred her view outside. She began to cry. "Mommy, Daddy, Charlie, please come home fast!"

Lightning flashed. Thunder crashed nearly overhead. "Dear God," she murmured, "please bring them home *now*!" Another lightning bolt, and a strike of thunder shook the house. Tears ran down her cheeks, matching the rivers streaming down the window. She turned and ran to the closet to hide, all the while pleading, "Mommy, Daddy, Charlie, God, somebody!"

Feeling alone as she never had before, she huddled and cried in the corner of the closet, as far from the window as she could, for what seemed forever. She tried to remember something her grandfather had often quoted: "Hope deferred makes the heart sick, but when the desire comes it is the tree of life." Something like that; she tried to think comforting thoughts of Grandpa cuddling her on his lap. Her tears subsided, but she couldn't stop trembling.

The long moments trailed, and then she heard the patter of footsteps on the sidewalk, and the front door bursting open. Daddy's deep voice and Mommy's tinkling laughter rang out, and then, "Ivy—we're home!"

The girl named Ivy jumped from her closet hiding place and streaked across the bedroom floor to greet her soaking-wet family who had finally returned home.

Section 2: On the Odder Side

RAIN CHECK

The trail beneath the sky-blocking hemlocks leads me to a clearing where an outdoor restaurant has been carved into the rain forest. Is it a mirage? The Rainy Café beckons me with its red cedar tree at the center of a stone patio. I walk over to the tree and estimate its trunk is twenty-five hands around. An 'elf's doorway' in one side is a clue the tree is hollow. I must take a peek inside to see if there is a skylight above the gnarly branches of this massive tree. There is—and at almost high noon, sunrays slant down, capture and illuminate dancing dust motes and spider webs. The pungent odor of cedar holds me as I take a deep, satisfying breath.

A hunger pang reminds me it's time for lunch! No other customers have yet entered the Rainy Café, and there is only one table in the circular patio. A metal pedestal table is covered with a red-checkered cloth, and two white chairs sit at skewed angles beside it. A sign on the table reads *Reserved*. A white china dinner plate anchors the tablecloth. A scattering of crumbs indicates someone has finished a meal. So perhaps *Reserved* no longer applies. A brown cafeteria tray lies on the ground beside one of the sprawling chairs. One edge of the tray shows teeth marks. Hmmm … Someone must have been really hungry! Or maybe a teething child took comfort bites. At least the last customers were neat, except for the crumbs. And the plate licked clean! Or so it seems.

No waiters have shown up, so I take a chance that the reservation party has already lunched. I position one of the garden chairs at the table and sit down, placing my backpack on the other chair and scooting it tableside. The sunshine is warm, a light breeze whispers from the forest, and I pleasure in the scents of moist earth and rain-soaked wood. Makes me feel sleepy ….

My eyes pop open. Still, no other guests have arrived— odd at noontime! And even stranger: no waiters have come out from the small concrete-block building to provide a menu and perhaps a welcome glass of ice water. That would taste so good after my trail hike! Now I'm really thirsty too! I sit waiting, my feet enjoying a rest, toes wiggling in my laced-up hiking boots. I am alone at a restaurant on the edge of a mighty forest! I hope someone else will appear. The breeze changes direction, turns chilly as it curls inside my shirt collar.

After a while I hear a rustling sound in a nearby thicket and turn to look. A black bear shambles out from a covering of berry bushes and staggers toward the table where I'm sitting! The hairs on its head shimmer like gold threads in the sunlight. Why do I notice that? My brain trying to stay rational, while I'm frozen in place, terrified? The bear moves closer; I smell a light musky scent and see horrible, long claws attached to monstrous paws. And teeth like daggers! But is the bear grimacing or attempting to smile? It tilts its head, looking at me as if interested— kindly almost. A deep growl erupts from its throat, then I hear clearly formed words: "This table is reserved."

The Rainy Café is obviously not what I expected, so I grab my backpack and hurry back into the safety of the dense, dark forest, leaving the bear to lunch alone. And myself to wonder: What just happened? I was hungry and tired. Delirious too?

HOOFBEATS OF DESTINY

When a herd of cows rushed into the yard, Tom Smith's political speech halted. In that moment when the picnickers froze in panic at sight of the stampede, Tom admonished over the microphone, "Run for the hills—it's the Jack Milton campaign!"

I was among Tom's followers who rolled off our hay bale seats and crawled under the wooden planks that formed tables. Farmer Mike Riley, host of the political shindig, had apparently lost track of his dozen or so dairy cows, supposedly fenced off in a distant pasture. Wild-eyed, embarrassed, and enraged, Riley was not far behind the cows. A black and white border collie yipped along at the farmer's heels. But the damage had begun. The country fiddlers fell off their metal chairs on the raised platform and fled for cover with the Democrats in shirtsleeves and summer dresses.

Folks will remember this on Election Day, I mused, cowering knee to knee with another young woman in a mini-skirt. *Maybe Tom Smith himself had opened the fence for the cows? Naw!* The 1966 mid-term election probably needed something to draw attention. *But not this!*

Tom Smith, age 25, was launching his first campaign for U.S. Senate to unseat the Republican incumbent. People thought this ambitious, energetic young man from Tipton, Iowa, had a fighting chance to unseat his opponent (*with or without cows.*) Polls showed that President Lyndon Johnson's Great Society programs were popular, and the Democrats expected to hold the majority in Congress. Surely, Jack Milton, with his limited-government ideals, was out of favor with the 'shared benefits, shared responsibility, equal opportunity' sentiments of the day.

From my crouched position under the makeshift table, I heard hoof beats above my head. *Would the boards hold a cow if it climbed onto the table?* I looked out from under a drooping plastic tablecloth to see brown and white cows at other tables lapping up beer from spilled cups and upsetting platters of jello—beautiful rainbow colors of jello, encasing bananas, shredded carrots and pineapple, fruit medleys of all kinds. At the dessert buffet, I watched the sacrilegious smashing of cakes—multi-layered beauties sprinkled with coconut, rich devils-food cakes slathered with fudge or butter cream frosting, upside down cakes topped with maraschino cherries. The cows were doing hoof paintings with these colors and textures on the wooden tables. The mess, of course, dripped between the planks onto potential voters. *Dear lord!*

The cows ignored the partially devoured steaks on paper plates. After all, they weren't cannibals! However, they seemed well disposed toward the jello. Baked potatoes wrapped in foil were nibbled at. Red, white, and blue balloons popping like firecrackers and the wails of frightened children added further sound effects to the melee of crashing cattle.

Farmer Riley and his dog ran about, attempting to corral the errant herd. The dog seemed more focused and in control than Riley, who flailed his arms and yelled a lot. Finally, the dog, with Riley's assist, got the cows lined up beside the beer barrel, where their great tongues beat at the spigot and lapped from the yeasty-smelling puddle on the ground. As the cows were having their fill, the guests gradually came out of hiding, many laughing.

A mortified Farmer Riley hailed an apology at the crowd as he led his wobbly cows off to their pasture, with the dog barking orders. I watched them head off across the dusty road toward a freshly-painted red barn where a banner proclaimed *Tom Smith for U.S. Senate.*

July's campaign picnic ended with Tom, his campaign staff, the musicians, and other good Iowa folks cleaning up the mess from the bovine invasion and restoring scattered American flags. I heard our irrepressible candidate chuckle as he made good use of a familiar quotation, "To the victor go the spoils."

Although the newspapers would have fun with this fiasco, I hoped the cows hadn't spoiled Tom Smith's political future. We were to find out on Election Day, November 1966.

MISTAKES WERE MADE

Windshield wipers swished back and forth. Jane's perfume clung in the humidity of the closed car. Ben's knuckles clenched the steering wheel, and he felt the urge to sweep away the curtain of water challenging the wiper blades on high speed. "What a night for a prom!" he muttered. "Why did we agree to this?"

"I know," sighed Jane, her corsage of baby roses drooping wetly after the couple's dash to the car. "Miserable, to say the least!"

"Hard to see anything; it will be even worse after dark," said Ben. "I worry about the kids driving in this, so young and inexperienced."

"Let's just hope it clears up." Jane squinted through the windshield. "What was that by the road?" She jerked forward, then twisted around to look back as their Corolla passed by a disturbance partly in the roadway ...."Ooh—you know what I think it was! A dog! Can you stop?"

"Not safe, can't pull off," Ben responded, tightlipped.

Jane doubled her fists. "You know we can't leave it there!" Ben's jaw tightened, as Jane continued, her cheeks turning red, voice raised a pitch. "Please, Ben—you know you'll feel bad later if we don't stop."

Ben, a small animal veterinarian, and his wife Jane, a science teacher at Garnet High School, were on their way to chaperone the senior prom at a Grange hall twelve miles out of town. It had been raining steadily all day, and rivulets of water coursed along the shoulder of the highway.

"Look for somewhere to turn around," instructed Ben.

Fingers to her mouth, a frown creasing her forehead, Jane peered through the oncoming rain. "There! Just ahead—looks like a driveway."

Ben tapped the brake pedal, checking for headlights in the rear view mirror. "Okay. I see it." He slowed the car nearly to a stop and turned right onto a lane. And then, they felt the car sliding and a sickening thud, as the tires refused to proceed. "We're stuck I think."

Jane was silent a moment. "What now?"

Ben shook his head, exasperated, then pounded his fists on the steering wheel. Jane watched him. He turned to her. "Well, Jane—you might have to drive in reverse while I push."

"O...kay," she said.

"Here goes—I'll be a sorry sight at the prom, but—well here goes!" He opened his door to a torrent of rain and a swoosh of cool air.

Jane squirmed across the gear shift levers to the driver's seat. "What do I do?"

Ben hollered back, "Put it in neutral and steer while I push it backward—and just hope nothing's coming down the road."

* * *

The compact car wasn't mired too deeply, and Ben felt it cooperate as he rocked and pushed it backward. "Now in reverse! Give it some gas!" he shouted to Jane. She followed his directions. Ben watched her back the car across the highway and stop, facing the way they had come. He trudged forward to catch up, sliding as the mud sucked at his dress shoes. Reaching the roadway, Ben realized he was unfit to be seen at the prom—or even to enter the car—but he felt grateful for the safety of no traffic in either lane of the highway.

He hastened to approach the passenger side of the Corolla and opened the door to hear Jane's outburst. "Oh no! Look at you!" Mudcaked shoes, saturated blue suit, red necktie bleeding onto his white shirt, hair plastered to his head and dripping.

Ben looked down at himself, shaking water off his hands. "I can't get any wetter. Let's get the dog. Move it Jane!" She glanced in the rearview mirror, shifted into *Drive*, and moved the car forward.

In a few moments, Ben said, "I hope you're okay driving. You sure wouldn't want to sit in this seat now."

With a half smile, she assured him. "I'm okay. The rain seems to be letting up a bit."

"About time," breathed Ben. They drove on. "The dog wasn't too far back. Along here someplace." He scarcely dared to think how or where Jane would manage to pull over to rescue the dog. Getting stuck again was a real possibility. "It's on your side now, so get a good look."

"I will." Jane bit her lip. She slowed down, checking for traffic behind, but there was nothing in sight. They soon came upon the heap by the roadside; Jane pressed on the brakes. "Oh my god!" she said.

By then, fully on the shoulder of the highway, lay a large cardboard carton marked *Made in China,* with frayed sleeves of a tattered denim jacket reaching out. "Someone's trash! I'm so sorry, Ben."

No reply. Ben eyed the distance ahead. Jane drove on as pellets of rain continued battering the car, and the windshield wipers kept up their rhythmic beat. Ben hugged himself. "I'm getting cold. Let's go back home so I can change clothes."

"Good idea," agreed Jane. "I'll keep going."

They returned six miles plus a few yards home, all the while Jane repeating, "I'm so sorry." She said it again as they pulled into their driveway.

Ben grabbed her arm. "Enough Jane! You were right. I couldn't have left a dog out there in pain. It was an easy mistake; we could hardly see what it was. Now let's find me something else to wear to the prom."

Jane's smile brightened her face; her shoulders relaxed. "Okay. Still sorry."

"Don't!"

As they entered the house, the phone was ringing. Jane ran to answer it in the kitchen as Ben ran upstairs. "Hello! ... Julie—what are you doing? ... Chemistry homework? ... Why aren't you at the prom? ... It's *next* Saturday? ... Oh!"

FOSSIL FIND

Willard was more myth than man. No one had seen him in eighteen years, but he was thought to live alone in the Sheraton. The Sheraton Forest, that is—a deciduous hardwood forest remnant above the Missouri River that the pioneers had left intact after hacking away the rest for lumber and firewood. Songbirds and raptors inherited the stands of oak, hickory, and cottonwood, some Scotch pine, and floodplain shrubs. It was true that Willard called this forest his home. As for forest remnants, he might be mistaken for one who'd lived during early settlement days, with his long gray hair in mats, wrinkled leathery face, and tattered clothing hanging in rags around his strong thighs.

Willard's house—a shack, to be generous—resembled a turtledove nest with its boards and tree branches haphazardly tossed and stuck together. It held up well enough, with regular adjustments by Willard. Somehow, this modern-day pioneer had picked up clues about structural engineering.

Stories about the Hermit of Sheraton Forest, who lived by his wits and Nature's grace, circulated through each new freshman class at nearby Pioneer State University (PSU): Some said he was the descendant of a fur trader and his half-Indian son who were buried in the forest. Others told of the wailing cries of banshees or wolves emanating from the forest at night, although wolves were never spotted in the daylight. Other tales circulated about PSU coeds who had disappeared near the forest. Credible accounts reported occasional explosive noises from the forest after dark.

Fascinated by these stories, enthusiastic students in small groups sometimes set out to find the mythic hero, but over the years, no one had wandered far enough into the forest to stumble upon Willard or his eclectic hideaway.

Besides, would his home be recognized as anything but an enormous rat's enclave? The recluse's natural alarm system enabled him to hide upon the approach of humans. His winged friends, the crows, warned him of intruders long before Willard could see or hear anyone coming.

* * *

A resourceful PSU geology professor, Dr. Rock Armstrong, during his second year of tenure, discovered a promising new source of fossils. A layer of limestone filled with traces of Paleozoic sea life appeared in the cliff face beneath the Sheraton Forest where deposits of windblown loess were eroding. One morning toward the end of spring semester, Professor Armstrong invited his Saturday students to be the first to explore this promising ribbon of fossils. From a rock-filled draw at the cliff's base, it would be an easy climb of about twenty feet to the fossil band and a shelf from which to work at dislodging fossils.

Fifteen students chipped and picked at the limestone to uncover brachiopods, corals, and trilobites, once alive in an ancient sea. About noon, when the professor left to go on a run for watermelon, just up from Texas at a nearby farmers' market, five of the students (two guys and three girls) surprised the others by scrambling up the cliff, using the cat-step features of the loess to reach the top. From above they hollered down to the others. "Come on up—it's way cool!" called Matt, flapping his t-shirt to let in air.

From the ground, Wendy tossed her maroon-tinged hair and yelled back, "You know you're already in trouble. Can you even get down?"

Matt laughed. "Piece of cake!"

His blond buddy Jeff stood next to Matt and pulled something out of his shirt pocket, waving the objects in the air. "With these sticks we won't have no problems." Matt lurched to grab at one of Jeff's marijuana joints.

The girls—Carol, Samantha, and Amy—were dusting off the powdery loess soil from their legs below their shorts.

Carol looked over at the guys. "You came up here to fire up? How lame! I'll bet we could do something more fun."

Samantha suggested, "We're in the Sheraton Forest. What say we look for The Hermit!"

Amy seconded the idea. "Come on!"

"Don't get lost, girls," teased Jeff, lighting one of his joints.

As the girls plunged into the forest, following a wildlife trail, Matt expressed concern to Jeff. "We'd better see where they go—just in case."

The five students wound their way through limbs and underbrush, scratching their bare legs, except for Matt in his sturdy jeans. Samantha and Carol trekked in flip-flops; Amy wore tennis shoes and socks that attracted sandburs. As they followed the trail deeper into the forest, the friends exchanged stories about The Hermit. Matt, at the back of the group, plugged his iPod headphones into his ears and marched to his own drummer for a while.

At a division of the trail, Jeff announced, "Decision time!" Laughing, "I'm going to blow another stick. Don't know what the rest of you're gonna do!"

The students stood gazing at where the path divided. "Let's stay together, whatever," Amy said shakily.

"I agree," said Carol. "Let's just pick a path and all of us go."

"But leave a marker," said Samantha, "to find the main path again." She looked around and quickly found two rocks to pile on top of each other at the base of a tree. They set off again, with Matt grooving to the music on his iPod and Jeff, half stoned, tripping along behind the girls.

Whether it was the scent of marijuana smoke that drew him or the failure of crows to warn him, suddenly Willard appeared, walking down the trail toward the students. He stopped; his eyes popped wide open. The students held their collective breath. Could it really be? The Hermit of Sheraton Forest!

Jeff's eyes glistened as he stepped forward to greet the strange man emerging like a vision from the forest. Jeff raised his hand, palm forward. "Howdy!" Willard turned away.

"No! Come back," pleaded Samantha, whose idea it had been to find The Hermit.

At the sound of her feminine voice, Willard hesitated and faced the intruders. He made a grunting sound.

"Can you speak?" asked Samantha, inching away from her friends toward the recluse clothed in rags.

He made another sound that came out like "huh?" As Willard began backing away, Samantha in her bright yellow t-shirt and denim cutoffs, slowly extended her hand as if to calm a stray dog. He looked at her sunny face and outstretched hand and began to smile, revealing a wreck of jaundiced teeth.

Willard motioned for them to follow him, and so they tramped along behind the foul-smelling man, to his nest of tree branches and planks. He motioned proudly toward his burrow and beamed his chipped teeth again. Carol and Amy turned away from him and made a face at each other; Samantha held her nose and looked inside the Hermit's hut. There wasn't much to see except a bed of leaves and ferns and a Mason jar of ancient vintage half full of liquid, probably rainwater. There was no sign of food, but a rusty shotgun and a slingshot were evidence that the hermit hunted his meals.

Jeff looked around outside the shack and noticed a patchy cultivated area. "What're ya growin'?" he asked Willard. "Ditchweed? Good stuff?"

The Hermit shrugged as if he didn't understand Jeff's question. "Don't be crude," Carol said to Jeff. "These look like edible plants—maybe like wild lettuce or roots."

Jeff laughed. "Just hopin' and wishin.'"

Suddenly Willard walked over to Matt and looked sympathetically at him. The Hermit touched one of Matt's earbuds. Then he motioned to his own mouth and shook his head. "Hear no evil, speak no evil," Jeff interpreted. Matt smiled, took out one of his headphones, and held it up to the older man's ear.

Willard heard music for the first time in eighteen years, yet music unlike the hits of the 90's. He smiled and rolled his eyes.

Jeff was inspired to share his marijuana with The Hermit; he handed the joint to Willard. "Have a hit!" said Jeff. The recluse took a couple puffs. Again, he smiled and rolled his eyes.

"Better than candy," said Willard.

"You can speak!" gushed Amy, running over beside Willard. He looked at Amy, his clouded eyes under shaggy brows tracing her body from head to legs. There he stopped and pointed to her patched and frayed jean shorts. Then he motioned to his own garb and smiled. Amy laughed at the comparison.

Jeff commented, "You're stylin', man!" The students laughed, and Willard did too, the sound bubbling up from his throat like waves over rough rocks.

Then Willard asked a question, "PSU?"

"Yes, yes!" The girls exclaimed.

"Me too," said Willard. He pointed to his chest where a faded *PSU Engineering* was barely visible on the shirt that seemed pasted with sweat onto his body. The students peered at the markings.

Jeff clapped Willard's back, and they all gave a cheer for "Good ole PSU!"

"And we should get back," warned Amy.

"Professor Rock will call out the troops," agreed Matt.

So the five students bid goodbye to Willard. On the return hike along the trail to the loess cliff, they discussed whether to tell the professor, Wendy, and the other geology students about their encounter with The Hermit of

Sheraton Forest or whether to keep him as their secret fossil find. Carol suggested, "We could be famous for actually spotting the Hermit after all these years."

"And ruin his privacy forever," noted Samantha.

"We didn't even find out his name," said Amy. "We should have."

"Go back!" said Jeff, looking over his shoulder at the girls. "Go back and ask him."

The girls stopped walking. Matt, in the lead, turned around. "Don't be crazy. These paths can be tricky. I'm not even sure we're on the right track to get back."

"How far along did I leave those rocks?" asked Samantha.

Amy fretted. "We're lost and I really have to pee."

"Me too," said Carol.

Samantha, hands on hips, sighed and gave them a hopeless look. "Complications!"

"Well, just go pee!" said Jeff.

"Not here!" said Amy.

"We won't watch," said Jeff, turning his back. Matt laughed.

"We'll go off a ways," said Carol. "Don't leave this spot!" She warned the others.

"I'll come too," said Samantha.

"Don't get poison ivy on your butts!" called Jeff, as the girls wandered off. Two crows flew out of a spruce tree, cawing, as Jeff's laughter echoed.

With the girls out of sight, Jeff said to Matt, "We could actually leave them." He chuckled.

Matt frowned. "You're crazy, man. Why would we do that?"

"Cause I'm hungry. No time to waste."

"You're nuts. You won't be much hungrier when we get back to the dig."

"I need a smoke then." Jeff reached to the back pocket of his cutoffs where he carried a plastic baggie containing matches and joints. "Hey—it's gone! Where's my sticks?" Jeff checked the other back pocket, the ones in front. Searching, panicking, Jeff said breathlessly, "We gotta go back."

"Hold on," said Matt. "Don't go berserk on me. Just look around here; they probably just dropped out."

"We need to re-trace our steps until we find them."

"It's not life or death," Matt assured him. "You can get more."

"I'm going back," said Jeff.

Matt grabbed his arm. "No!"

Jeff shrugged off Matt's grip and dashed into the forest, back down the barely-worn trail.

"Jeff! Come back!" Matt shouted to the trees. But Jeff was gone.

When the girls returned, Matt was standing alone. "I'm glad somebody came back!" He grinned sheepishly.

"Where's Jeff?" the girls said in unison.

Matt nodded toward the shady forest they'd passed through. "He lost his joints."

"Oh, for goodness sakes," said Amy. "Now what do we do?"

"I'd vote to leave the bastard here," said Matt, "but—"

"We could go back toward the Hermit," suggested Samantha. "It's not that dark yet." The afternoon sun winked at them through the tops of swaying tree branches; shadows were growing longer.

"Maybe we could just stand here and wait for Jeff to come back," noted Carol. "We've come this far and I hate to lose our progress."

Not far down the trail, a group of three or four crows swooped out of the cottonwoods, heading toward Willard's camp. "Wait! I smell something," said Samantha. "Smoke!"

"Pot smoke?" asked Amy, sniffing.

"Kinda smells like it," said Matt. "Let's follow our noses." He started down the path. The girls followed.

They pushed their way into the deeper forest, not talking, hearing only their breathing and the soft sounds of their feet pounding the earthen floor. The aura of smoke through slanted sunbeams drew them on. "This trail's looking a little familiar now," Samantha suddenly spoke.

"Yes, it is," agreed Carol.

Then, they saw him: Jeff popped out of hiding behind a tree trunk. "Glad to see ya!"

"What in the—?" began Matt.

Jeff shushed him with a finger to his lips. Whispering, he said, "Just a ways farther on, the guy's in his hut smoking—"

"Marijuana?" asked Amy. "All that smoke?"

"Yeah. But he had something else on fire too when I got here."

"Now what?" said Matt, raising an eyebrow at Jeff.

"Well, now that yer all here for backup, I'm goin' after my sticks," said Jeff.

"Wait, wait—what if he—" began Matt.

"He'll have to give them back—with all of you here."

"Do you think he found your joints or stole them?" wondered Carol.

"Doesn't matter." Jeff shook his head.

"Maybe it does," Matt disagreed. "We don't know what he'll do."

"We need to be careful," warned Amy.

"C'mon." Jeff stomped off toward Willard's camp. The others followed, cautious paces behind.

They came upon ashes from a smoldering fire and bits of bone and unidentified furry skin. A few yards farther, the students crept up and saw Willard's feet sticking out from his shelter. Perfect smoke rings circled above, as Willard seemed to be relaxing after a meal. "Aha!" shouted Jeff.

There was a skittering notice inside the hut, and Willard emerged to face the group. No one spoke until Jeff told the man, "I came back for my cigarettes."

Willard simply stared. As Jeff rushed toward him, Willard moved away toward some scrub trees, where his shotgun rested. Jeff glanced inside the shelter. On the bed of leaves he saw the baggie with the matches and two joints remaining. Jeff crawled in and grabbed the bag. As he rose up out of the entrance, the Hermit faced him with the rusty shotgun pointed. Amy screamed. "Put down," demanded Willard, indicating the baggie in Jeff's hand.

Jeff, his face pale, looked over at his friends. They stood watching the stalemate. Jeff sunk to his knees on the ground. "Man—I need these," he pleaded.

"No," said the Hermit. "Willard need!" He cocked the shotgun, ready to fire.

"Willard!" Samantha called out. "Is that your name?"

The man lowered his aim slightly and turned to Samantha. She forced a shaky smile. Once again, she extended her hand to the shaggy recluse. "Willard?"

He kept looking at the girl in the yellow shirt and denim cutoffs, wearing flip flops for shoes. "Willard need matches," he said.

Jeff raised his bowed head. "If I give you the matches can I have my joints back?"

Willard aimed the gun at Jeff again. "Take smokes. Put matches in house."

"Thank you. Can you put the gun down now?"

Willard waved the gun. "Matches in bag—in house," he warned.

"Okay." Jeff took the two joints out of the plastic sack and put them in his back pocket. He showed Willard the bag still containing matches, then tossed it into the hut. "Okay, now?"

Willard nodded and smiled his corn-colored teeth.

"Can you put down the gun?" begged Jeff.

"Go now," ordered Willard, motioning with the shotgun toward the way out of the forest.

Jeff got off his knees and joined his friends. "Let's go!" He was shaking, as was Amy. Their feet tumbled together as they fled Willard's camp.

A short way down the now more-familiar path, Matt said to Jeff, "I hope you're happy." Jeff didn't reply, and the girls remained silent.

A little farther on, they heard a shout from Willard's location. "PSU!" Then a gunshot exploded, reverberating through the tranquil forest.

"Man," said Jeff, "that thing really was loaded!"

The sun was dropping relentlessly into the west when the students found the rock markers Samantha had left by the tree. As they walked the last tenths of a mile to their starting point, Amy said, "Well, at least we found out his name."

ECLIPSE OF THE YELLOW BALLOON [2]

"It's been a perfect night," I told my husband, John, as we sat together on backward-facing seats on the MAX train headed west. We were leaving downtown Portland after a wonderful evening of dinner—with dessert—and before that, a walk along sidewalks lined with massive old trees splashed with fall color.

John squeezed my hand as the train lurched and rocketed forward. "Happy birthday again." He smiled.

"You know, what really tops it all is the total eclipse of the moon on my birthday night." I reminded him, "I did tell you there was a total eclipse the night I was born too."

He nodded. "I seem to recall that."

I looked at my watch. It was just after 8 o'clock. "It should be happening already." I craned my neck to catch sight of the eclipsed moon out the window. But the well-lit interior of the train compromised the black sky. All I could see were reflections of us passengers. Soon we were plunging into the darkness of the long tunnel that zoomed us through to Washington Park. As we finally decelerated into the Sunset station, John and I peered out the windows for a glimpse of the moon playing peek-a-boo with the trees.

We reached our destination at 185th Avenue and finally caught a clear view of the sky and of the Hunters Moon, eclipsed by the earth's shadow, dusty gold in color. We stared for a few moments to get an eye full of this miracle of nature, as the moon would soon move out of the shadow to shine brightly again.

---

[2] Unlike the rest of the book, this story is absolutely true!

Walking toward our car in the parking lot, I noticed a round object, glowing yellow, in a grassy area near the sidewalk. It seemed that a small moon had touched down during the eclipse. I went over and saw that the orb was a yellow balloon, almost fully inflated, its string caught under a wooden bench. In spite of John's quizzical expression and head shake suggesting *no,* I rescued the balloon and brought it into the car. "It's a symbol," I explained. "It's my birthday balloon—and nearly the color of the eclipsed moon tonight."

"Okay." He nodded and started the car.

I brought the balloon home, where it mostly settled down into our downstairs family room. Sometimes the balloon rose off the floor and soared with air currents; it spun around the room as our grandsons circled it, their little hands batting and capturing this magical toy. The balloon was a hardy player, always ready to bounce and roll or just sit quietly when no one was around. Luckily, our cat was afraid of it. When she snatched at the string, the yellow balloon moved ever so slightly and warned her off.

The balloon spent Thanksgiving with us, Christmas, and New Years. It seemed to love celebrating and was always lively at parties when anyone wanted to play catch or parade it through the house. My birthday discovery lightened and delighted my heart as it did the night I found it at the MAX station during the eclipse. Sometimes I would look at our round yellow guest and marvel that it never got smaller. I wondered how long it would stay, how many more play dates and holidays it would spend with us.

Then, one Saturday in early February—just before Valentine's Day—John was running the vacuum cleaner in the family room. The balloon was lounging on the floor near the fireplace. The machine got too close to the balloon, and with a horrible screech, sucked up the string. A resounding pop signaled the balloon's demise.

But the yellow balloon wasn't finished! It took its revenge by breaking the vacuum cleaner. My apologetic husband took the vacuum apart, tried to screw it together, sweated hard, until he was no longer sorry but angry. He had to take the appliance to a repair shop. The experience was a reminder that one should be cautious running a vacuum cleaner within range of a very special birthday balloon.

BANANA FOOLERY

A gorilla ambles into the Safeway Store, snatches a shopping cart, and heads over to the produce aisle. He bellies up to the banana display and begins loading bunches into the cart.

That was an April Fools prank I'd dreamed of pulling off in college but never did. Last year, I mentioned the idea to my wife Marcy, and to my surprise, she said, "You should do it!"

"Huh?" Well, okay, so I began to think about the joke again, despite being no longer a kid.

To prepare, I joined Marcy at her yoga class for six months and limbered up. I gradually became flexible enough to bend over and touch my toes. After the first five months, I could even do the gorilla pose, reaching hands under feet all the way to my wrists—quite a feat for the hamstrings! After all this preparation, I figured I could lope into Safeway and walk a short distance on feet and fists, like an ape.

The gorilla suit was expensive, even to rent. It looked real—excessively hairy—and stank inside of nervous perspiration; it hung heavily on my body. Luckily, April Fools Day in Portland wouldn't be hot. I could live in the shaggy, airless costume for up to an hour, probably.

The big day arrived! With a boost from Marcy, I donned the suit. The oversized feet felt strange, even though the inner linings fit like slippers. Marcy helped me stagger to the car as I got used to lifting ape feet. I didn't wear the headpiece with gorilla mask while in the car for fear of freaking out another driver. Until ...

"Watch this, Marcy!" I said as we drove up beside a car full of teenagers at a red light. I ducked down and quickly pulled on the gorilla head, and then I rose up and looked out the passenger-side window. A horrified teen girl's face looked back, quickly morphing into a laughing face, then fingers pointing, the teens' car rocking with laughter.

As we pulled away from the stoplight, Marcy checked the rear view mirror. "They're following us." Apparently, the teen driver had swerved into the lane behind us. We turned into the Safeway parking lot, and Marcy noted, "They're still following."

"Of course, wouldn't that be the normal teen reaction?" I said.

"Just wish you hadn't surprised them, Jim."

"Oh well. After all, it *is* April Fools Day." The knowledge that I already had an audience gave me added incentive to pull off my long-dreamed-of prank.

Marcy dropped me off at the south entrance to Safeway. She would park, and then quickly follow me at a discreet distance with our video camera.

As I walked toward the automatic door, a woman with a little girl stopped abruptly, watching me and protecting the child with one arm. As I went to grab a shopping cart, I sensed blank air around me, no other persons coming near. I yanked a cart by its handle with vigorous gorilla strength (thanks, yoga class!) and wheeled it around toward the nearby produce aisle. An elderly man in a gray jacket stood watching me, open-mouthed. I nodded politely to him and proceeded on.

The woman at the florist kiosk saw me and uttered an amazed "Oh my!" I hoped Marcy was not too far behind, catching these reactions. And where were the teenagers?

Minding my gorilla business, I arrived at the banana counter and began heaving bunches of bananas into my cart. From the corner of my eye, I noticed the familiar produce man stop sorting avocados and dash away toward the back of the store.

Finished emptying that bin, I spied another heaping counter of bananas under the *organic* sign. While pushing my cart forward, I bumped some organic cabbages off another counter, and several wrapped balls of cabbages rolled across the floor. Here was a perfect opportunity to practice my gorilla walk, so I bent over and shambled on all fours to retrieve the cabbages. (*Marcy, are you getting all this?*) I didn't see her, but hoped she was recording the video by this time.

As I reached around a corner of the low counter to pick up a cabbage, I came eye to eye with a mini-shopper. He screamed "Mom?" I cocked my head in a friendly way and looked at the boy. He surprised me by picking up a cabbage from the floor and handing it to me. I accepted it with an extended ape hand and wanted to say *thanks*. Instead, I grunted in my best gorilla imitation. The boy ran off. I replaced the cabbages and headed for the organic bananas.

One glance, and I saw Marcy peeping over the lemons, trying not to look conspicuous with the camera. The teenagers were over by the apples, giggling, as they looked my way. I began tossing the organic bananas into my cart. It was now full, and some bunches were balanced precariously atop the load. Then, it dawned on me, *what am I actually going to do with all these bananas?* I guessed I could either go to the check out and pay for them or start putting the bananas back where they came from.

I didn't have to consider the question for long. Two policemen were advancing toward me, followed by a very red-faced produce man, followed by a man in a shirt and necktie who I perceived was a store manager. "What's this all about?" a husky, young policeman asked gruffly. His thinner, even younger, sidekick stared me down.

"April Fool?" I chuffed in my best gorilla voice.

The officer had a citation book and pen in hand. "Do you know it's only March 31?"

"What?" How could Marcy and I have messed up on the date after all our careful planning! "Are you sure?" I was then so hot I had to remove my gorilla headgear.

"Yep," said the policeman. His partner nodded. "Now, if you'll put these bananas back where you got them, there will be no charges." He turned to the produce man and manager. "That all right?"

The manager said, "Sure, fine, okay."

Marcy came over and grabbed my furry arm. The policemen tipped their caps to her, and then walked away. "I got some great video," she whispered into my sweaty neck.

The teens came over to help us restock the bananas. "Great joke!" one boy said. "Too bad it was the wrong day."

I shrugged and tried to smile. "Guess that makes me the April Fool."

TWO SHORT AND SWEET

A Drabble and Tweets

HEART-STOPPER [3]

I ripped open the mail:

Dearest Dear—Every night around eleven, I drive by your house, hoping to catch your perfect form on the window blind. Look out and watch me, watching you. Wave if your husband is gone. I will rush to your waiting arms, as I've wanted to for so long ….

In shock, I sat down at my kitchen table, the letter fluttering in my shaking hands. It appeared I was being stalked! Turning the envelope over, I saw it was actually addressed to my next-door neighbor.

Sometimes we learn too much about our neighbors!

---

[3] This short fiction is a drabble—a story containing exactly 100 words.

FIRST TWEET

GEORGE WASHINGTON ON TWITTER [4]

On Seeking First Presidency Of The United States

- I really wanted to retire to the plantation, but if my country needs me I will seek the presidency. Cherry trees can wait. LOL

- Some fear I would be another King George. Not my intention to begin a dynasty. I haven't the teeth for it.

- 12 candidates. Most votes wins presidency; second will be VP. Lincoln? Clinton? Adams? Me? Hancock a big name too.

---

[4] A tweet is an online posting on *Twitter*, each tweet limited to 140 characters or less.

On Life As President

- New York, Philadelphia were OK capitals. But my dream to build a special capitol comes 2B when I lay the cornerstone in '93.

- Another portrait sitting! That makes 19, not including sculptures. Wasn't one enough? Artists need to make a buck.

- My tenets: A strong federal government, central bank, standing army, religion free and separate. Any questions?

- Jefferson and his crowd don't like my ideas of strong central government. IMHO, Jeffersonian states' rights will lead to trouble.

- Martha and I need a vacation, but nothing foreign. Maybe a nice little cruise down the Delaware—remembering.

Section 3: Long Story Short

IN CASE OF FIRE

"Damn door," sputters Annlee Malcolm. A wheel of her wheelchair bangs against the unyielding oak doorframe of the closet. She grunts and gives the wheel another jerk. Under her crown of grizzly over-permed hair, she thrusts out her lower lip in a determined pout. "Stupid wheel!" She is stuck inside this enclosure in the rear entry hall. She knows she's being childish to hide here, but she knows why: Since she was a girl growing up in this great house, this closet has been her storm shelter during scary electrical storms and her deaf father's yells rolling like thunder through the mansion. *This is my house, and I'll do what I damn well want to!* She can even say 'damn' to herself. The wheel remains caught on the oak door, as Annlee kicks the door with a foot trapped in a brown oxford. Cocker spaniel Missy, Annlee's aged soul mate, clings to Annlee's lap, toenails embedded in the edges of her rolled-up nylon hose. Gray wiry-haired Scotty barks beside them. Annlee reaches down to him. "Shush!" She knows the dogs have never got used to these plunges into the closet beneath the back stairway, nor her temper tantrums.

The mulish wheelchair scrapes and thuds against the doorway. Scotty wiggles free past the apparatus. Then Carla, one of the housekeeper-aides, comes to assist. Her bony hand reaches toward Annlee's chair. "Here, Miss Ann. Let me help you." Annlee is relieved when Carla frees the wheel blocked by the doorframe. She rolls her eyes at the way Carla always smells of tuna fish and wears that god-awful hairnet.

"Is the storm over yet?" demands Annlee, peering up at her aide.

"It's over."

"Good. That was a pleasant start to the day!" says Annlee in a gloomy voice. Scotty barks and paces around the wheelchair. A ray of light slants through the windowpane of the back door onto the yellow-flowered wallpaper. Carla wheels Annlee along the hardwood floor to the living room at Bluebird Hill. Rusty and gray-tinged Missy rides on Annlee's lap; they both stare straight ahead to the pillared porch framing the outdoors.

"I'll be getting your lunch ready soon, Miss Ann," says Carla, whistling lightly through her chipped front tooth. "I tole you I won't be staying the night, didn't I."

"Yes, you said," replies Annlee, eyes downcast.

"I'll stay into the afternoon, maybe get you settled back in bed before I go."

Annlee harrumphs.

"You know I can't stay nights by myself. An' Ellen can't be here tonight."

"Oh, go on," grumps Annlee, her voice husky. She knows that the help—Carla especially—are frightened to stay alone at night in this slate-gabled mansion overlooking the Ohio River. Carla is not even brave enough to hunker down in the 'fortress' in the wood-paneled kitchen and butler's pantry where Ellen, another helper, has parked a single bed and lamp table between the 1970s refrigerator and a recent-model washing machine. Annlee listens as Carla explains that Willy Leerman and his wife are just a phone call away in the carriage house. Annlee knows this, but she doesn't interrupt, realizing that Carla is trying to assuage her guilt and cowardice in not staying overnight in this house of creaks and groans."Yes, I know. I know," growls Annlee, "I'll call the Leermans if I need to."

Carla directs Annlee's wheelchair to her mahogany library table by a porch-side window. "Stop," demands Annlee, as they cross the faded oriental rug covering the warped floor. Annlee doesn't want to sit at her table cluttered with gift catalogs and scraps of paper. This morning she prefers to wander on her wheels around the enormous room while Carla prepares lunch.

"All right, Miss Ann," Carla sighs, "lunch will be ready soon." She lets go of the wheelchair and retreats to the kitchen. Annlee sighs. *Tuna fish again!* Scotty dances around his owner's rig, and Missy climbs arthritically to the floor. Annlee makes an effort and grabs at the wheels to move forward. She feels different today—prepared and resigned to spending the later hours of this day by herself, accompanied by her four-legged companions. She has a premonition that tonight there will be more violence in the atmosphere—an eclipse to the morning's thunderstorm.

Annlee has been expecting to hear from her nephew Bob Malcolm, even though last month a Jefferson County judge issued an order against Bob's contacting his aunt in any manner. Annlee senses he might try something soon. For one of the rare times in her eighty-nine years, Annlee feels she has some control—at least over her emotions, simply by being prepared for the worst.

Ghost voices of a meeting just five months ago still echo in this room, but Annlee cannot hear them distinctly ….

* * *

That anguished day she had hidden away in her bedroom with Missy and Scotty when the lawyers, Judge Steven Beer, and Annlee's nephew Bob came for the house tour, led by Howard Michaels, the gentle handyman who was overseeing band aid repairs to the house. The visitors braved the overwhelming stench of dog urine and feces that had been absorbed into the floorboards and carpets and steeled themselves for what they might observe.

In the dining room, Bob was saying, "You can see putting $250 thousand into this house is a waste of money." He spoke to the judge and, indirectly, to Judith Amadeo (Annlee's attorney) and Edward Bock (attorney for the bank). "Just look at that hole in the ceiling—and a bucket on the floor to catch leaks!" Stocky white-haired

Bob raised an arm in his tidy dark blue suit and shook his fist at the ceiling. Turning to Howard, he pointed to the gaping hole. "What'll it take to fix that? Is the sub-structure of the roof involved?"

"Probably," Howard said in a low voice, tugging on his plaid golfer's cap.

"And what is being done on the outside—on the roof?" Bob persisted.

"All the tiles need replacing. It's still the original roof up there," said Howard, adding that at some point in repairing the roof, plumbing, and various beams and structures, "we could hit asbestos. We're not sure what to expect. And with the number of gables—"

"You see!" said Bob to the group, straightening his necktie.

Judge Beer, in his mauve and black striped polo shirt and Reeboks, was taking careful notes on a lined tablet. Bob continued talking. "And another thing—as far as taking funds from my grandfather's trust, my aunt can't control her spending. She doesn't know the value of a piece of paper!"

Judith, in her flower-print ankle-length dress, shifted her weight to one hip. "Now that's an exaggeration, Judge," she blurted.

Bob continued, "For instance, what has happened to all the furniture in this room? There have been a number of things removed from this home. If my aunt sold them— where's the money? Things have walked out of this house."

"Okay. It's true," snapped Judith. "There's furniture missing but that's not really the issue here, is it!" She clicked her heels on the bare wood floor and walked straight out of the dining room. Judge Beer followed her, and the others followed the judge.

The real issue at hand was a request for an encroachment on Annlee's parents' estates left in trust for her, particularly her father's—the Lee Robert Malcolm Sr. Trust—the principal of which would be left to Bob after his aunt's death. It was now worth over $3 million, and Bob wanted desperately to protect it. He also had his sights on the ten acres plus of Bluebird Hill real estate, which he contested should be part of the Malcolm Sr. trust and not Annlee's personal property. Court-ordered permission to encroach on the trust principal was requested by the bank and Annlee's attorney Judith, as monthly income from the trusts continually fell short of costs for extensive house repairs and Annlee's growing medical and home health care needs. As yet, no one had been successful in getting Annlee to stop her catalog ordering; gift buying for friends and workers; and charitable gifts to wildlife organizations, churches, civic groups, and more.

The house tour pushed onward, up the stairs past a stuffed toy black Labrador lying beneath the grandfather clock, only to be challenged by a croaking plastic frog beside the next step—a catalog gem that gave Annlee a rare chuckle whenever a guest was surprised. This group, vaguely amused, proceeded upstairs and searched through non-working bathrooms and antique bedrooms, looking at more peeling plaster and water damage. Judge Beer ran his fingers along windowsills and opened closet doors. "What skeletons are in here?" he charged, laughing.

The judge, ever diligent in his examination for the court, pointed out doorbell-like ornaments on one of the bedroom ceilings. "What are those?" He turned to Howard. "I've noticed them in all the bedrooms up here."

"I believe those are fire sensors," attempted Howard, looking up. But he didn't know exactly how they worked— "Probably one of those later inventions they added onto the house during the 1920s."

The judge rubbed his chin. "But some of these have been painted over. Any idea why?"

Howard said, "I'm guessing the system isn't working by now."

Leading the procession up a narrow stairway, Judith proclaimed, "The attic—the best for last!" The others allowed Judith to open the door to the attic. "No one had entered here until last week when I came up here with Howard and some of the workmen," stated Judith. "Everyone was afraid of raccoons but none were found." She let fly the door for the others to feast their eyes on old suitcases and gnawed patches in the walls where the night creatures had previously let themselves in.

Returning to ground level and going down to the basement, Judge Beer continued questioning Howard and making notes. The judge ignored the combative legal chatter between Judith and long-haired, stoop-shouldered Edward; he stopped listening to Bob's complaints about how his grandfather's mansion had fallen into ruin as if it were his personal loss. The judge kept writing.

In the basement, the tour group splashed through water, stooped under pipes and ductwork, asking Howard the usual, "Where does this go to?"

Good-humoredly Howard would occasionally say, " I really don't know. I'll have to look into that." At one point, Judge Beer peered into a crawl space to look for termite damage and Howard warned, "Watch your head."

One of the surprises in the basement amid cobwebs and old pipes and boilers was a recently installed alarm system. The group stopped to look at the incongruous red shiny box in this gray space. "I had that put in a couple years ago when I was helping my aunt," claimed Bob, assuming a proprietary tone.

"Does it ring in directly to the fire department?" said Judge Beer.

"No. It connects to a central point, like ADT, and the alarm goes out from there," Bob responded.

"It's not plugged in," Howard pointed out.

Judge Beer stopped writing. "Why?" No one spoke. The judge began tapping with his pencil on the note pad. The others stared. Edward crossed his arms and looked thoughtful. "This makes me wonder again about those outdated doorbell fire sensors we saw upstairs," said the judge. "I think the first thing to be done is to get this system connected back up."

* * *

Annlee stares up at the great clock on the stairway landing. The toy black Lab on the steps is a reminder of the many dogs of this breed who had been her companions through life. Most of them are now buried with her pony in the rose garden across the driveway from the back entrance. Annlee raises her eyes up the stairway and peers into the darkness where Judge Beer and the others had trod. Annlee can't go upstairs anymore, but from those steps, sixty-five years ago, she made her entrance as a debutante, dressed in pink chiffon and wearing three strands of pearls, her light brown hair in a stylish bob. *I felt like a fool—too old really for the task at hand, but Daddy made me. And my escort—that puny, bald runt—just because he worked at Daddy's business. And a bachelor— ugh!* Annlee laughed out loud, a spiteful laugh, as she remembered: *Making my debut got me one decent date— only one—what was his name?*

But ten years later, Annlee recalls, she descended the stairway as a bride to meet the love of her life, Tom Dolan. Her eyes sweep around the living room where their wedding took place. Garlands of white roses and shiny leaves wound along the stairway banister, the fragrance of magnolias flooding the living room. Tom, dark hair slicked back and neck flushed above his shirt collar, wore a white carnation in his lapel. *Before that I loved roses, but from that day on carnations have been my favorites.* Now, from her wheelchair, she looks over past the sofa, its worn chintz covering reeking mercilessly of dog urine. She stares at the white tile fireplace where the wedding vows were recited. The half-columns on either side of the fireplace mimic the columns of Arlington, the home of General Robert E. Lee, depicted in the oil painting above the mantel. *My family always seemed to need big houses!* Scotty distracts her for a moment as he runs, barking, toward the door to the porch. "A squirrel, Scotty?" *Maybe a deer,* she considers before resuming her memories of the wedding day.

Yes, in November that year. Everyone, especially Mother, beaming with happiness. Everyone, except him! She refers to her late half-brother, Bob's father, who had expressed anger when the engagement was announced. Annlee found out later that her half-brother Robert's disapproval stemmed from a fear that any children from this marriage might endanger Robert's inheritance from their wealthy father Lee Robert Malcolm Sr. *As if there wasn't enough for everyone. One thing good about my father, he was rich. The Malcolms are a greedy lot!*

Annlee doesn't question her own mind, but in recent months, inchoate thoughts about her husband, long dead, have pushed to the forefront of her consciousness. *Tom!* Turning her chair slowly toward the dining room, she tries to shake off painful thoughts of her beloved and what all too soon followed the beautiful wedding. *I'll come back to that later,* she thinks, as if there is something that needs finishing. Meanwhile, taking inventory around the main floor of the house will distract her. She glances again at the painting of the Confederate general's famous home, nods her head, and pushes into the dining room. Missy is close beside her while Scotty stops to pee on a corner of the sofa.

She gazes into the sparsely furnished dining room. The bay window with a view of the river seems a long way across the room. Uneven, shabby window blinds and rusty radiator covers beneath the windows diminish the pleasant vista beyond. Paint and plaster peel around the yawning gap in the ceiling, exposing floor beams above. Beneath the hole, a white plastic bucket sits half full of water. *How does water find its way there from the outside?* Annlee shakes her head. In the center of the room a card table is covered with a white cloth, hand-embroidered purple Irish bluebells adorning the scalloped edges. She remembers her mother doing embroidery under a dim lamp as Annlee perched on the arm of a tall chair. Her mother's missing dining table used to seat up to twelve guests for her famous dinner parties. *Some of those were fun, with cousins.* Now the Duncan Phyfe chairs are gone too. *I loved those little lyres in the chair backs. What ever happened to the furniture?*

She vaguely recalls a time in the recent past when she was quite ill in her bedroom on the other side of the house, she heard footsteps tromping through the hall and beyond, maybe going in and out of the dining room. Heavy sounds of furniture squeaking and dragging across floors came through her fevered fog. And she remembers Carla's continuing references to "Back pay, what you owe me, Miss Ann." *Did that really happen or did Bob take the furniture?*

Carla comes into the dining room with lunch on a tray—a tuna sandwich and steaming, aromatic tomato-basil soup. "Can you come over to the table Miss Ann?"

"Yes, I'm getting there," says Annlee, wheeling herself over from the fireplace.

Carla sets out the food, and then leaves Annlee in the empty dining room to eat her lunch and wash it down with a coke. Annlee eats and shares bits of her meal with Missy and Scotty. She notices that the equestrian-patterned wallpaper is in a peeling stage after so many years. *Was that on the wall when Tom and I married? I guess so.* She is drawn back to reflecting on her short marriage to Tom Dolan, four years passing with him in the War in the Pacific with never a furlough, his changed personality upon return, the divorce. She has always blamed her half-brother Robert for manipulating those events—perhaps getting Tom drafted in the first place, or writing threatening letters to

Tom, or arranging to have his leaves canceled. She doesn't know what really happened. But Annlee knows that her half-brother wished to destroy her marriage. *And he did! Those Malcolm men always get their way.*

* * *

Nephew Bob is no exception. Now, in his late sixties, Bob is shorter than his father Robert had been, and more robust than was Lee Robert Malcolm Sr. Bob has a southern-gentlemanly air belying a ruthless nature. He has been trying for over twenty years to obtain money from Annlee's father's trust. First, he tried to convince the bank to lend him $100 thousand from the Malcolm trust for his son's college education. Bob argued it would be no different than any other investment the bank would make on behalf of the trust—and wasn't education the best kind of investment after all! The bank was sorry but they couldn't agree.

Next, Bob tried to get the bank trust officers to take over management of his aunt's financial affairs, fearing she was severely overspending her income and would eventually deplete the trust principal. The bank sent cajoling, then warning, letters to Annlee but didn't solve the problem as Bob saw it. He threatened to sue the bank. Annlee continued spending in excess of her monthly allowance from the bank, as the dining room ceiling crumbled with no funds to repair it. So Bob presented a disability petition to the court, stating that Annlee was delusional and incompetent to handle her own affairs. Bob asked to be appointed her legal guardian with power of attorney. Judith's legal skills and a letter from Annlee's doctor, declaring her mentally competent, had put an end to Bob's plot to control Annlee's money that time.

In his most recent attempt, Bob fought the current request for the $250 thousand encroachment from the trusts. Judge Beer ended the case, after the house tour with the attorneys, Bob, and Howard the handyman. The judge ordered the bank to invade the Malcolm parents' trusts for the requested amount. The funds were to be applied to a list of needed house repairs and handicap accessibility updates, but no paved path to the rose garden and pet cemetery. The encroachment would also include funding for Annlee's medical needs and salaries for the home care workers. All parties, except Bob, viewed the judge's decision as even-handed.

One of the last statements Bob had made to the judge was "That house should be burned to the ground and my aunt placed in a nursing home. We'd all be money ahead." As a second thought he added, "and my dear Aunt Annlee would be better cared for."

Annlee had told Judith she knew Bob would try another approach to get "his" inheritance. "He'll probably try to kill me," said Annlee, half-joking. Judith reported to Judge Beer that Annlee was in fear of her life from Bob Malcolm; the judge issued the restraining order against him.

* * *

Following lunch, Annlee leaves her dishes on the card table for Carla to pick up. "Come on Missy. Come, Scotty," she encourages, wrists aching as she tries to back up her wheelchair. She can't manage to go the way she wants. "Dang fool chair!" She rings a little hand bell for Carla. Missy and Scotty start barking. Carla shuffles into the dining room. Her look of annoyance does not deter Annlee from giving orders. "I left the dishes on the table, and then will you phone an order to send flowers for Judith's birthday! Now, wheel me over to the library table." With an audible sigh, Carla obliges. "And some cleanup needed over there," commands Annlee, pointing toward the sofa where one of the dogs has left a "calling card" on the carpet. Annlee delights in making menial demands on Carla; she figures it's her caregiver's just punishment for the way she ignores the dogs' needs to go outdoors and then forgets to clean up the messes left indoors. Annlee knows Carla must tolerate her demands, since she needs the money.

At the library table in the living room, Annlee sets some catalogs to the side and looks out the window on clearing skies and hopes to catch sight of a deer or bluebird. On the heavily carved mahogany table is a framed photograph of some of her best friends—the firemen of the River Valley unit, Engine 20. She picks up the photograph and runs her index finger across the glass, focusing on each man's face. She stops at the images of the station's Dalmatian mascots. "Hi Chief, hi Cinder!" She blows kisses to each dog.

The desk blotter on the table is covered with spots—*Like the dogs!* Annlee chuckles to herself, *and this old green thing has been here since the fountain pen was invented!* It was here when she used to watch her mother writing letters in her neat, curly penmanship. An edge of brittle newspaper pokes out from under the blotter. She pulls out the news clipping and sees the headline; it calls up more memories: FIRE STATION ANGEL GIVEN HONOR. Annlee has read this article about herself many times, but not recently, so she skims the story again. It details how she was named an honorary assistant fire chief after nearly a lifetime of befriending this firefighting unit. For years she sent lavish gifts at Christmas and occasionally purchased furniture for the station. She still tries to commemorate each fireman's birthday with a card or gift. As a younger woman she sometimes attended firefighter picnics and regularly stopped by the station to say a special hello to the Dalmatians who quivered with delight to see her. The news photo shows her receiving a badge and white firefighter's helmet from the fire chief.

Annlee remembers that her devotion to the fire station troop began when, at about age ten, she witnessed an horrendous house fire atop the next hill. It happened at nighttime, the massive tongues of flame leaping toward the dark sky, sparks shooting up as the three-story house imploded. From her mother's bedroom window upstairs, she watched the firemen's silhouettes, like little black ants, bravely fighting the monstrous inferno towering above them. When she learned later that they had managed to save the entire family—and their dog—the firefighters became her lifelong heroes.

A long time ago, she muses. She sets aside the news clip and opens the drawer to take out her checkbook and gel pen, as she remembers, *Time for their monthly check.* Her good friends, the firemen, are also an insurance policy. Alone in this massive house, with so many rooms she can't access, the danger of fire is often in her thoughts. She is glad the firemen at Engine 20 are so nearby and only minutes away should the alarm system be triggered. But she wishes they would visit her more often and, maybe, take an inspectors' look around once in a while.

During the afternoon, Annlee writes more checks—to the World Wildlife Fund and the Nature Conservancy—and addresses birthday cards to two firemen. She looks out the window at the thicket of brush, maple and sycamore trees extending down to Bluebird Valley. She chats with her dogs and caresses their scruffy little bodies when they climb on her lap. The grandfather clock ticks the minutes and booms the hours. Annlee wheels herself to the far end of the living room to peer out at the closed-off sun porch. Old letters, catalogs, and a couple of dolls are piled on the assorted wicker and rocking chairs lined up around the streaked window walls. She doesn't want to open the door and let in the confusing scents of mold, dust, and ancient potpourri—faded dreams. She turns around and inches her way back to the library table, clicks on the shaded Tiffany lamp, puts on her reading glasses, and finds her page in *James Herriot's Dog Stories*.

Carla enters the living room. "I'll be goin' now Miss Ann. Shall we try to get you into bed first?"

Annlee looks over her glasses. "No."

Carla sighs. "I've laid out your nightgown on the bed. You can manage the rest, I guess. The potty chair is in the right place."

"Don't worry about me," says Annlee. "Maybe I'll still be sittin' here when you come in the morning."

Carla stares for a moment as if she'd forgotten something and bustles out of the room. In ten minutes she is back with a tray of food and a thermos of tea. Carla says, "You'll have to eat. Here's some fruit, banana bread, and tea—enough for all night if you need it." She places the food on the table.

Annlee smells the pineapple slices and just-peeled freshness of oranges; she feels a flicker of delight and manages to say, "Thanks."

Carla straightens up and looks over at Annlee. "If you need anything more—anything at all—if you want help gettin' into bed or anything, you can always phone down to Leermans."

"Okay, okay. I know." Annlee waves her off. "Good bye and good night."

"Good night, ma'am." Carla hesitates and then is gone, leaving Annlee, Missy, and Scotty alone on Bluebird Hill.

Most of her life, and especially since she lost Tom, Annlee has expected the worst—and lately the worst has happened, thanks to her nephew Bob's attempts to gain control of her life and finances. Annlee's premonition about impending trouble resurfaces in her mind. "Let it come," she says. *I'm eighty-nine years old and life isn't worth that much anymore.* Her feet and joints hurt, her stomach is often upset, cataracts cloud her eyes; she can't go anywhere. Tom and all of her contemporary friends are dead. Judith has re-written her will: her caregivers and the firemen are provided for; Bluebird Hill will become a wildlife preserve (the raccoons will have their day—and night). Annlee is satisfied, almost happy. She looks fondly at Missy and Scotty, both old too. "We'll stay together," promises Annlee.

About 11pm she hears glass breaking somewhere upstairs. Then more glass breaking. A little while later she smells something burning—definitely more acrid than a friendly log fire. From where she is sitting in the middle of the living room, Annlee sees a smoky haze filling up the staircase. She imagines the upper floor of the house on fire. The Leermans might be calling 911 right now, or the house alarm system will kick in, she thinks, alerting her friends at the fire station. *They will save us!* It would be a little while yet before the fire reaches the downstairs. Annlee takes a last look around. She wishes to save the Arlington painting; it has hung above the fireplace all her life, but she can't reach it. She wheels over to the library table and snatches up the photo of the firemen. Missy and Scotty begin barking; ears alert, noses twitching.

"Come on," says Annlee, heading for her shelter in the hallway. The dogs are close by her wheels, barking frantically. Annlee opens the sturdy door and slowly maneuvers just inside the closet. Missy runs ahead into the dark enclosure and sits looking out, long ears graceful and amber eyes aglow. Annlee and Missy look at each other; Missy has dislodged a cobweb onto her nose. When the lights flicker and go out Missy clambers onto Annlee's lap, bumping the frame of the firemen's photo. Scotty has scampered down the hallway toward the door to the outside and is barking ceaselessly. His little angled chin is profiled by a stray moonbeam coming through a pane in the door, and he paces circles within the hopeful ray. "Come Scotty, now," urges Annlee hoarsely. Then, "Are they coming Scotty? Do you hear someone?"

More barks, and silence outside the house. Crackling, breaking noises, muffled groans from the house interior. New smoky odors arrive in the hallway. Annlee notices her eyes are watering. "Please, Scotty, please come," she begs. Missy whines. And then Scotty whirls around and heads obediently into the closet. "Good boy," says Annlee, relieved. She tells her loved ones, "Help is on the way. They'll be here soon. They will find us in this closet." She inches her way into the musty depths and turns her chair to face the door.

* * *

Three fire engines move slowly down the service lane on Bluebird Hill, past the carriage house. The procession stops behind the silvery gray funeral car in the driveway. Fire Chief Stan Ellers, cap in hand, steps down from the lead fire engine from the River Valley unit and walks toward the funeral car. The funeral director, in black overcoat, opens the rear door of the vehicle for the firemen to lift out their heavy burden—Annlee Malcolm's walnut-finished casket, adorned with cascading red roses and white carnations.

Tearful Carla, the Leermans, Ellen, Judith Amadeo, Howard Michaels, Judge Beer, two neighbor women, and a newspaper photographer join the fire chief and more than thirty firefighters as Annlee's body, with Missy's and Scotty's, is carried to their final resting place in the rose garden where the other pets are buried. At the driveway entrance to Annlee's fire-smudged home, a bagpipe player intones *Amazing Grace.*

As the group of mourners cluster around the white picket fence enclosing the burial ground, Chief Ellers begins his address. "We are gathered on this beautiful morning to celebrate the life of one of our own. Annlee Malcolm was a good and true friend ...." A soft breeze stirs the sycamore branches towering over the garden at Bluebird Hill.

Made in the USA
Lexington, KY
29 September 2016